The Trench of the Dead

K McConnell

Published by K McConnell, 2024.

THE TRENCH OF THE DEAD

First edition. November 12, 2024.

Copyright © 2024 K McConnell.

ISBN: 979-8227277664

Written by K McConnell.

The Trench of the Dead
Part 1 – The Trench
1

The thumping of the helicopter felt like it was shaking every bone in her body apart. Even with the helmet on the pounding made it hard for her to focus. Outside the window snow swirled around them. They were flying through what they called a snow squall.

"Don't they heat this damned thing? I'm freezing." Jessica's voice came over the headset in Dr. Aurelia Moreland's helmet.

Before Moreland could answer her, the copilot spoke.

"Oh, sorry, Miss. We get used to it. I'll turn the heat up."

Moreland looked at Jessica. "Yeah. Everyone can hear you."

"Right." Jessica said.

Moreland hoped her decision to bring Jessica along with her on this was a good one. Jessica had a tendency to speak her mind as quickly as a thought came to her. Still, she was by far the most energetic of Moreland's graduate research assistants and she was hoping that energy would be useful to overcome some of the difficulties in a paleontological dig in the Antarctic.

The helicopter emerged from the snow squall into sunshine. The snow covered ice seemed to stretch on forever below them.

Moreland felt a little nervous. Not because she had been selected to take part in such a new and exciting endeavor as this, but because she hadn't spoken to Dr. Palfrey in several years. Laurence Palfrey was never known for being very social so it was no surprise that he had not contacted her much, but Moreland felt some guilt because she had deliberately not communicated with Palfrey.

Moreland had been an exemplary student at Harvard and knew she was lucky to do graduate work with Palfrey, one of the world's most prominent paleontologists, but she had aspirations of her own. Working as an assistant to Palfrey left her always feeling like she was laboring in the shadows. It was why she had chosen to take a position at the University of Chicago when she got her doctorate. Palfrey was not happy with her choice.

In spite of their limited communication over the past several years, Palfrey had sent her a letter asking her to join him here. It was the chance of a lifetime. The first substantial paleontological dig in the Antarctic.

The sound of the helicopter changed. Moreland couldn't see anything more than the empty snow from her window. To the south there was a massive jumble of ice. She wondered if that was man made. The ice that had been excavated to create the trench. She glanced forward past the pilot and copilot seats out the windshield. She could see a grouping of lightly constructed buildings and tents to the left and there it was. The Trench. Almost a mile long and as much as a half mile wide.

She stared at the massive gaping separation of the ice sheet that stretched out before them. It was truly astounding what they had been able to accomplish. An area of ice had been cleared out exposing long buried Antarctic ground. She knew there were mountains that stuck up above the ice, but fossils were not likely going to be found up on those rocky slopes. She also knew that there were other areas of the Antarctic where the ground was exposed or at least accessible, but this area they knew was special.

Technology was an amazing thing. Moreland, herself, wasn't much of a technology kind of person and as such did not understand exactly how this new "radar" worked. All she did know was that they had been able to use it to penetrate the ice here where it was thinner and see right into the ground good enough to actually recognize shapes long since buried. Those shapes, with the help of AI, strongly suggested bone structures.

The helicopter turned left towards the camp. Just outside the perimeter of the camp the helicopter set down. A couple of soldiers came on each side of the helicopter and opened the doors. Jessica and Moreland got out. They peeled off their respective helmets.

The cold wind blew past and seemingly through them. Instinctively both women reached back to pull their hoods up the block the wind. Moreland pulled her hood up past her black shoulder length hair that had been tied back in a short pony tail. Jessica's short blonde hair stuck out in wild directions. A gift from the helmet she had been wearing.

The soldiers escorted them over to another man standing nearby obviously waiting for them. By the way their escort soldiers saluted the third man Moreland assumed this was Major Wilkins.

"Dr. Moreland?" Wilkins held out a hand. His voice was raised to overcome the sound of the wind.

Moreland shook Wilkins' hand. "Major."

"You're late." Wilkins said.

"I didn't fly the helicopter." Moreland said.

Wilkins looked at Moreland for a moment. "Can you fly a helicopter?"

Moreland shook her head. "No. That was sarcasm."

Wilkins gave a brief smile and nod. "Right. Well, this way."

With a wave of his hand Wilkins turned and led them into the camp. They passed a couple of small buildings and into the central section of the camp where a mix of people walked and a variety of snow vehicles maneuvered around anything that got in their way.

Jessica's head swiveled as they walked trying to take in where she was at. Moreland wasn't sure where exactly they were going. Wilkins turned and led them into a building. It was nice to get out of the wind and into somewhere warm. It was the dining facility.

"Cup of coffee?" Wilkins gestured towards the cafeteria style bar that ran along the left side of the room. He had pulled back his hood to reveal black hair that was starting to show some gray. His features were sharp. A no nonsense look.

"That would be great." Moreland said.

"A shot of whiskey would be better." Jessica said.

Wilkins smiled. "That can be arranged as well."

"No." Moreland said in Jessica's general direction.

The door behind them swung open and they turned to see the same two soldiers that had met their helicopter carrying their bags. Moreland looked at the bags puzzled.

"Uh, Major...our bags? Are we spending the night in this camp?" Moreland asked.

Wilkins glanced back at the bags. He shook his head. "No. They'll go down on the lift with you."

"The lift?" Jessica asked.

"I thought the helicopter would fly us down to the lower camp." Moreland said.

Wilkins hesitated. He seemed to be a little confused and then a thought occurred to him.

"Oh, no. Can't fly the helicopter into the Trench. There's a perpetual fog down there. Too risky to fly down there." Wilkins said.

"What's the lift?" Jessica asked.

"We have a crane at the edge of the trench. We lower supplies or equipment down and anything or anyone that needs to come up with it." Wilkins said.

"A crane?" Jessica said. She was clearly not comfortable with the idea of that.

"How safe is that with this kind of wind?" Moreland asked.

Wilkins waved that off. "Oh, that's no problem. The wind dies out once you drop down past the edge."

Wilkins led them to the long food bar and he and Moreland got coffees. Jessica settled for a hot chocolate. They sat down and passed a little time in small talk.

"Your trench is much bigger than I thought it would be." Moreland said.

Wilkins nodded. "Yeah. The boys did a hell of a job on it. Took them weeks to carve it out. Good thing the ice is thinner here than most of the Antarctic or they would still be at it."

"Don't other parts of the land stick through the ice?" Jessica asked.

Moreland nodded. "Yes, but those are typically the tops of mountains. Not an ideal place to find fossils."

"Yeah, I guess, but when we flew in there were some areas with hardly any ice covering them." Jessica said.

"They used the new deep penetrating radar on areas around McMurdo in their testing. Didn't see anything of interest there I guess." Wilkins said.

"How deep is the ice here?" Moreland asked.

"About 100 feet. Give or take." Wilkins answered.

"Oh, I thought the new radar could only go down a 100 feet." Moreland said.

Wilkins shrugged. "I guess it depends. It seems to average around 120 feet. It will get through about 100 feet of ice and then it depends on the kind of material beneath that. At least, that's what they tell me. I think they said that the soil under this ice is largely...al...love..."

"Alluvial deposit?" Moreland suggested.

"Yeah, that's it." Wilkins said.

"Sandy stuff." Jessica said. She looked at Moreland and smiled. "Look at me, I remembered something from undergrad classes."

Moreland laughed a little. "I hope more than just that."

"Well, whatever." Wilkins said. "I still don't understand how anything could have ever lived in this place."

"Oh, well, the Antarctic continent wasn't always encased in ice." Moreland said. "It was much further north in the Cretaceous era. There was no ice here and the climate was temperate."

"Ah, OK. Well, we should probably get going." Wilkins said and stood up.

They left the dining hall and the brisk wind hit them as they walked out. Wilkins led them towards the Trench. They stared at the massive crane parked back from the edge of the Trench. In front of the crane was a large steel platform. It had a railing around the sides of it and the railings on two ends could be opened like gates. There were multiple places all around the floor and railing of the platform where cables, chains or straps could be attached.

"Wow, that's big." Jessica said.

"Yeah." Moreland nodded in agreement.

A couple of soldiers took their bags and strapped them along opposite sides of the platform. They stood waiting on the platform.

Wilkins turned to them. "They've got a couple of harnesses for the two of you."

At Jessica's worried face Wilkins held up his hand.

"Its just a precaution. Once the platform drops over the edge there should be very little sway to the platform." Wilkins said reassuringly.

"Drops?" Jessica said.

Wilkins smiled. "Just and expression. Gently descends."

"I like that better." Jessica said.

Moreland and Jessica stepped on to the platform and the soldiers helped them into the harnesses. A strap from each harness was connected to the platform itself.

Wilkins drew closer to the two of them so they could hear him better through a gust of wind.

"Now, there is a slight sway to the platform as it goes down. More so the further down you get, but nothing big. For safety's sake, please do not unclip the harness. Also, its best if you sit down on the platform. Don't worry. You'll be fine." Wilkins smiled at them and walked off the platform.

The two soldiers stepped off the platform and a rumbling sound came from the crane. Slowly the engine of the crane cranked up and then the platform lifted slightly. The moment the platform was off the ground the wind tried to push it.

Jessica shot a nervous look at Moreland. Moreland gave her a quick smile. It was about all the reassurance she could muster at the moment.

Before the platform could move much, though they saw the two soldiers holding cables at different corners stabilizing the movement of the platform.

Moreland felt her own wave of nervous tension as the crane eased the platform past the edge of the trench. Neither Moreland or Jessica was next to a side rail. They were both sitting almost in the middle of the platform. Moreland assumed that was maintain a certain balance to the platform. It did prevent them from being able to peek over the edge and look down. Moreland thought that neither one of them was likely to do that even if they could.

Some of their worries were tempered by the fact that the thick fog filling the trench below did not allow them to get much of a gauge on just how high up they were. It looked like they were floating just above a peaceful gray cloud.

Jessica's expression took on an even more worrisome look to it. Moreland turned her head around and saw that the platform must be hanging over the trench now. She could just see out of the corner of her eye Major Wilkins and the two soldiers manning the lines standing on the ice a short distance away.

The platform started down. It wavered some as it went and Moreland had to admit it gave her a little nausea at first. They had dropped down below the level of the ice and immediately Moreland could feel cold air behind her. She knew it was the ice wall sucking heat out of the air. It felt like being lowered into a giant freezer.

Suddenly there was an odd hissing sound and Moreland and Jessica looked at one another. They glanced around the platform, but nothing seemed to be causing the sound. Movement on both ends of the platform drew their attention. They saw the cables the soldiers had been using to control the platform drop past them. There was a gentle jerk as the cables reached their length and hung below the platform.

They had dropped down further before they could hear above them a gust of wind. It didn't reach down to where they were at, but it had an effect on the platform. They felt the whole platform turn slowly clockwise about 45 degrees and then stop and slowly spin back the other way. It repeated that several times before slowing down to an easy sway.

"I think I'm getting seasick." Jessica said.

"Hang in there." Moreland said. "This won't take too long."

"Can't be soon enough." Jessica said looking a bit pale.

Moreland smile. "Well, if you vomit over the side the people below are going to get a special kind of rain."

"It would serve them right for making me ride this damned thing." Jessica muttered.

They had dropped into the fog now and with every passing minute it was getting harder to tell how much progress they were making. The world around them was nothing but gray cloud. They lost a sense of how fast they were moving or how much time was passing.

When they hit the ground with a jolt both of them were caught by surprise.

"Ow!" Jessica exclaimed. "That hurt my ass."

Moreland rubbed her own butt as she stood up. "Yeah. They might have warned us about that."

Out of the fog that still encompassed the platform two people emerged. One, a tall man wearing a dark blue hooded coat. The man's hood was pulled back and his round head was mostly bald. Only sparse silver hair adorned the sides and back of his head. The other man was young. Clearly a soldier. His coat was lighter and of military design. His light brown hair stuck out from under a green cap.

"Welcome to the Trench." The tall man said stepping on to the platform and extending a hand towards Moreland. "I am Randolph Beecham. I kind of run things around here."

Moreland shook his hand. "Dr. Aurelia Moreland. Its not 'Colonel' or 'Major' Beecham or anything like that?"

Beecham shook his head. "No, Doctor. I'm just a civilian. I worked with Dr. Palfrey on another of his excavations so the military brass allowed me to manage things down here. Its mostly just administrative stuff anyway."

Beecham turned and waved towards the soldier that was with him. "This is Private Devon. He's going to help you with anything you need while you're here."

Devon nodded politely. "Ladies."

Moreland pointed at Jessica. "This is Jessica Samson. She's a grad student and will be helping out on the work."

Beecham picked up Moreland's bag and Devon did the same for Jessica. They all stepped off the platform and started walking.

"How do you know where you're going in this fog?" Jessica asked.

Beecham smiled. "Well, first you orient yourself based on the platform. It generally always lands in that manner. Then..." He paused as they took another couple of steps and a small orange flag stuck in the ground seemed to magically appear on cue. "...we follow the markers."

"Still seems like you could get lost here." Jessica commented.

"Yes." Beecham said. "Best not to wander too far off the trail. Worst case, though, you can always just call out. Sound carries really well down here and someone will hear you and shine one of the big flashlights to guide you in. It happens."

"Why do keep looking at your feet?" Jessica asked looking over at Moreland.

Moreland looked over at Jessica. "Just marveling at the ground."

The ground they were walking on was a mix of sand, gravel and chunks of ice left over from the ice removal. It was gray and brown.

"Its dirt." Jessica said.

"Dirt that hasn't the light of day since this continent drifted to the south pole." Moreland said.

Jessica glanced down at the ground. "OK. Old dirt."

Their arrival at the camp was kind of sudden. They could hear some sounds from the camp as they approached it, but had not actually seen anything. One moment it felt as if they were nowhere and the next tent shapes and vague moving figures were all around them.

Beecham veered right and stopped in front of a tent.

"This is you." Beecham said. He pulled one of the front flaps aside.

Moreland stepped in first followed by Jessica.

"Its bigger than I thought it would be." Moreland said looking around. There were two cots, two tables and a chair for each table. There were also footlockers under each cot.

"Its...more 'tenty' than I was envisioning." Jessica said.

Moreland glanced over at Jessica. "The Hilton was all booked up."

Jessica shot a quick glance over at Moreland. "They have a Hilton here?"

Moreland just stared at her.

"Oh, right. Sarcasm." Jessica dropped her pack next to a cot.

"Do you need some time to settle in or would you like to walk out to see Dr. Palfrey?" Beecham asked.

Moreland eased her bag down next to the other cot and walked back out of the tent. "I would like to check in with Laurence, Dr. Palfrey."

"Very good." Beecham said. He turned to Devon. "I see the tent has not been stocked with the basics. Can you see to that?"

Devon nodded. "Yes sir." He gave a courteous nod to the women and disappeared into the fog.

Beecham led Moreland and Jessica across to the opposite side of the camp and then out along another marked trail. They walked for about a half mile before they started hearing muffled voices.

Jessica stared at the fog around them. "Is it always this foggy?"

Beecham shook his head. "No. It varies some. There is always some fog, but sometimes its not as dense as this. It seems to be linked to high and low air pressure fronts. It's just up here. Hopefully Dr. Palfrey is in a good frame of mind today."

"Oh?" Moreland said. "Is anything wrong?"

Beecham shrugged. "I don't know. I mean, no, nothing in any practical sense. Dr. Palfrey seems to be disturbed about something with the data on the fossil site. Doesn't make sense to me. He is complaining about there being too many potential fossils in one location. He thinks the data might be wrong."

"Too many fossils?" Jessica asked.

Beecham nodded. "Yeah. Go figure. You'd think a paleontologist would be thrilled to find a big pile of bones."

Beecham zeroed in on Palfrey's voice. They came upon a gray blob that finally dissolved into three people. Palfrey and two soldiers. One of the soldiers coughed loudly.

"You verified the distances with the laser tape measures?" Palfrey's voice was asking. He had the appearance of a cartoon rendition of a mad scientist. His white hair, while not long, stood up and twisted in all directions. His equally white mustache and goatee adorned a face that seemed a little gaunt.

"Yes sir." One of the soldiers replied. Both soldiers held some red reflectors and laser range finders.

Palfrey stood on one side of a folding table upon which were several large printouts and a tablet designed to be used out in the field.

"OK. We have the extended area to the north that still needs to get laid out and there is still some of the overburden to be cleared there. You can work on that." Palfrey said. He heard them approach and turned. A wide smile crossed his aging and lined face. His gaze was entirely on Moreland. As an afterthought he glanced quickly back towards the soldiers and waved them on their way. They nodded and disappeared into the fog.

"Aurelia." Palfrey said and hugged her.

Moreland felt a little awkward. She had never been accused of being overly affectionate. She had several failed relationships in her past as evidence to that fact. Also, she was still harboring some guilt for not being better at staying in communication with Palfrey.

"Doctor." Aurelia said as they parted. "It's good to see you."

"It's wonderful to see you." Palfrey said. "Your timing is perfect. We have already cleared the initial overburden and we are just now hitting the fossil rich layer."

"That's amazing." Moreland said.

Palfrey nodded. "Indeed. Its very exciting. This new USR technology is incredible. It has allowed us to zero in on both location and depth to a degree that has sped up the process 10 fold."

"USR?" Jessica asked.

"Oh, I'm sorry, Doctor, this is my grad assistant Jessica Samson." Moreland said.

Palfrey smiled at Jessica. "Very pleased to meet another generation to our honorable cause. To answer your question the USR, uh, Ultrasonic Radar, can penetrate quite a ways into the Earth and return a 3D map of what lays beneath. Its amazing. The material densities, chemical signatures, ah, millions of data points."

"Wow, sounds like a lot of info." Jessica said.

"Indeed. That is why we had to employ AI to sift through it, based on our criteria, for what locations held the greatest likelihood of holding the fossils we seek." Palfrey said.

"Sounds wonderful." Moreland said.

"Indeed. Let me show you where we are at in the primary site." Palfrey turned.

"Dr. Palfrey," Beecham stopped Palfrey, "they have only just arrived. Perhaps we could do this first thing tomorrow."

Palfrey looked confused for a moment. Clearly his excitement over what they were about to embark upon had separated him from some basic realities. He hesitated and then nodded.

"Yes. Of course. You are correct." Palfrey glanced off in the direction the soldiers had disappeared into the fog. "Ah, those boys know what they need to get done."

Palfrey rolled up the printouts on the table and tucked them under his arm. He scooped up the tablet and together the four of them walked back to the camp. Scattered lights began to appear out of the fog as the daylight started to wane. There was a light on a tall stake in between each tent. There were also numerous reflectors around the camp. There was a variation in the colors and Moreland was sure the colors signified something.

In camp Palfrey told them he would meet them in the dining tent. He had to drop off his stuff in his tent.

Beecham led them to a larger tent towards one end of the camp. When they walked in Moreland immediately recognized it. The dining tent. It was set up identical to the one up above. They got in line for food and then sat down at a long table. Palfrey joined them a few minutes later.

While they ate, Palfrey explained that the Army had supplied all the manpower he needed to get some of the initial digging done. Just a thin layer of overburden. Finer excavation now was needed to start sorting out what they were looking at.

"That's just amazing how this radar technology has sped the process up in finding fossil specimens." Moreland said.

"Yes, well, we certainly have found a mother lode of specimens." Palfrey said, but his expression seemed subdued.

"You're not happy with the progress?" Moreland asked.

Palfrey glanced up from his plate at Moreland. He waved a hand. "Oh, I am, it's just...I don't know. It seems odd. So many in one area.

Clustered so tightly together. I've never seen or heard of a density of this magnitude before."

"Well, the Burgess has a pretty high concentration." Moreland pointed out.

Palfrey nodded slightly. "Yes, but those species, 450 million years old, are fairly small in size. The event that buried them had a much greater chance of catching a significant number of specimens in a given area. The size of the specimens here is much larger. It's obvious a cataclysmic event buried these fossils, but, I don't know. So many animals of this size in one location and by location I am referring to an area of a size heretofore unknown in the history of paleontological sites."

"It sounds like this is the opportunity of a lifetime." Moreland said.

Again Palfrey nodded slightly. "Yes. I just wish I could understand what brought so many animals into one general area at one moment in time."

"Well, perhaps when we sort out how many different species we are looking at it will help point to a reason for their presence here in such numbers." Moreland said.

While they ate people, some soldiers and other civilian staff, came and went. Throughout the ebb and flow of people there seemed to be the steady sound of occasional coughing.

"Yeah, we do have a bit of a cold virus running through the place." Beecham commented when he noticed Moreland glancing around at the sniffles and coughs.

"I guess that goes with the territory living in a refrigerator." Moreland said.

After dinner Moreland and Jessica returned to their tent. The day's travels were starting to take their toll on the both of them.

Someone, presumably Private Devon, had provided them with some basic essentials, Kleenex being one of the more important items. The cold air tended to make one's sinuses run some. Also, the small gas stove for heating had been running which helped to mitigate some of the chill.

Jessica plopped down on her cot. "Is that humming sound going to go on all night?"

Moreland sat down on her own cot. "Those are the generators. Without them we wouldn't haven't any electricity."

Jessica just looked at Moreland. "So...is that a yes?"

Moreland unlaced her boots and laid back on the cot. She was very tired. "Yes. That's a yes."

Jessica still sat on her cot. "Did you notice the smell? It really kind of stinks here. Doesn't it?"

Moreland took a deep breath. She was worried she had made a mistake bringing Jessica along. Jessica was a promising student and Moreland felt that this would be such a tremendous opportunity at an exciting experience.

Moreland let her breath out slowly. "The smell most likely comes from the newly exposed microbial material in the soil. Its been frozen in ice for millions of years."

"OK. Old microbes." Jessica said.

2

They sat across from each other in the dining tent. Moreland sipped her coffee and watched Jessica shoveling in scrambled eggs, some kind of bacon substitute and a glass of orange juice. Ah, Moreland thought, the days when you could eat without thinking about calories or cholesterol or anything else. She glanced down at her banana and yogurt.

Jessica was talking between mouthfuls about Harlon, her part time boyfriend back at the University and how she didn't think she could trust him and she knew his sister and she said...blah, blah, blah...

Moreland chose to listen to the soldiers sitting at the next table. While it wasn't an exciting conversation by any means, anything was better than...

"No. Didn't show up for duty this morning. Sarge is out tracking him down." The soldier said. She waved a disgustedly hand.

"Wilson said he was feeling like shit last night. Barely ate anything." Another soldier added.

"Barely does any shit anyway." A third soldier said. All three laughed.

Another soldier leaned over from a different table. "You talkin' about Wilson? I saw the Sarge helping him over to the Admin tent just a few minutes ago."

One of the soldiers started to say something, but broke into a coughing fit before he could speak.

"Good morning. How was your first night here?" Beecham asked walking up to their table.

Moreland looked up at him. "Fine. Thank you."

Jessica waved a hand at Beecham while the other hand pushed a piece of fake bacon into her mouth.

"Well, as usual, our esteemed Dr. Palfrey is already out at the site. I suspect he may have gone out there before it was even light out." Beecham said with a smile.

Moreland nodded. "OK. Well," she glanced over at Jessica, "as soon as the food runs out in here I am hoping we can be on our way."

Jessica stopped chewing and looked at Moreland and Beecham for a moment. She shrugged and kept on chewing.

It was another twenty minutes before Moreland and Jessica were working their way along the tents on the opposite side of the central walkway from their own tent looking for the blue reflector Beecham had told them to follow. When they found the reflector they turned right moved off into the fog.

The reflectors were positioned near enough that it was hard to lose track of them. In addition, there had been enough foot traffic moving out towards the site over time that one could almost find it just by following scuffled path in the dirt.

They had left the camp behind them and were now isolated in a foggy world of their own.

"This fog is just creepy." Jessica said.

Moreland laughed a little.

Jessica looked at her. "I'm serious. It is creepy."

"Sorry." Moreland said. "On a Fall week when I was a grad student, Laurence, Dr. Palfrey, asked me to join him on a quick trip to Newfoundland. He had this obsession that the area in Newfoundland of the Laurentian Shield should hold some specimens of early Cambrian fossils. You know, like the Burgess Shale. Anyway, we spent the whole week scrambling over rock outcroppings and every day looked about like this." Moreland waved at the fog around them. "But, what do you expect—-Newfoundland in the Fall."

"Didn't that get on your nerves?" Jessica asked.

Moreland shook her head a little. "Not as much as Laurence's frustration at not finding a damned thing. Most of the rock there is like 2 billion years old. Not going to find much of anything in that."

They walked on for a few more minutes before they could start to hear Palfrey's voice. They followed the sound. When they came upon Palfrey they were a little surprised to find no one else with him, but he was talking nonetheless.

Palfrey had his back to them and they watched him silently for a moment. He was bent over the ground with a tape measure and jotting down some numbers on to a small pad paper.

"For God's sake man, its basic geometry. Think. The diagonal has to be 22." Palfrey said disgustedly.

"Good morning." Moreland said.

Palfrey turned to look at them. "Ah, there you are. Excellent. I have an area plotted out for us."

Palfrey turned and glanced back at a stake and then back at the women. "Well, mostly marked out."

Moreland wander out into the closest area Palfrey had marked out. She squatted down and scanned the immediate area.

"I can see some interesting objects even at this level to begin excavating." Moreland pointed at a couple of different spots where a darker object seemed to slightly protruding from the soil.

Palfrey stepped a little closer to where Moreland was. "Yes. I had to restrain the boys when I set them to clearing some of the surface away. They were going to go at it with mattocks and pick axes. They would have shattered God knows how many specimens."

"This...seems surprisingly shallow." Moreland commented as she stood up.

"Yes. We saw that in the USR data. It is interesting." Palfrey said. "Come. I will show you where I thought we could start the initial work at."

Palfrey showed them the boundaries of where he wanted to start the more detailed excavation. He gave them a quick tour of the equipment locker stationed just outside the dig perimeter. After that they determined where each of them would begin work and they settled into some of the preliminary soil removal.

Initially as they worked Moreland and Palfrey talked about what each of them had been involved with over the last couple of years. Jessica listened in at first and then got bored. She just focused on what she was doing in the hopes that she didn't do something stupid in front of Dr. Palfrey.

Eventually the conversation turned to Palfrey explaining some of the process the Corp of Engineers went through clearing the trench out. The initial use of explosives to punch down through the ice down to within about 10 feet of the soil.

"I had a bit of a time explaining to the Army why blasting close to the ground level could damage the fossils. As shallow as they appeared to be I couldn't take any chances. They weren't very happy because the last 10 feet, without blasting, was a labor intensive process for them." Palfrey explained.

"Well, given how shallow these fossils are and the concentration of them we ought to be able produce a considerable number in a short period of time." Moreland said.

"I agree." Palfrey said.

"I wonder, though," Moreland said, "why not not bring in a larger crew? Given the volume of what's here."

Palfrey shook his head. "A large excavation is a lot to manage. More than that, when I studied the USR printouts the uniqueness of this site...well, there is something special about this place. There is a mystery here. Something I don't believe anyone else has encountered before. Too many people pulling lots fossils out all at once I believe we would lose track of the clues to solving what went on here."

After consuming a packed lunch that Beecham had sent out to them via Private Devon they worked through the long summer afternoon making good progress on exposing fossils in their individual work areas.

As they were wrapping up their respective work areas Jessica wandered over to where Moreland was working. She looked Moreland's work and then over at what Dr. Palfrey had accomplished.

"Uh, my area must have stiffer dirt than yours." Jessica said.

"What?" Moreland asked. "What do you mean stiffer?"

Moreland glanced over at Jessica's area. There was considerably less fossils excavated.

Jessica looked guilty. She glanced at her area and back at Moreland. "Stiffer dirt."

Moreland looked at Jessica. "It can take time to get a feel for this. But...you were on a dig last year."

Jessica shrugged. "Yeah. I did some digging and then they decided I was better suited to plastering the fossils for transport."

Moreland sighed. "Well, consider this a chance to brush up on your excavating skills."

"Right." Jessica said.

The three of them walked back through the slowly swirling fog to camp. A short time later they met back up in the dining tent.

"You know other people need to eat too." Moreland said glancing over at Jessica's well provisioned tray as they both moved along the cafeteria line.

"Yeah, of course." Jessica said with a casual shrug. After a moment she looked over at Moreland. "Wait. What are you saying?"

Moreland shook her head. "Nothing. Never mind."

Moreland sat down at a table across from Palfrey. Jessica sat down next to Palfrey whose tray was only sparsely populated.

Moreland looked at the contrast of the two trays.

Jessica watched Moreland's eyes travel from one tray to another. "What?"

Moreland shook her head. "Nothing."

"You aren't eating much." Moreland said to Palfrey. "Are you feeling OK?"

Palfrey waved off the question. "I am fine. Just...thinking about the dig."

Moreland nodded, not completely convinced. "Have you been able from the USR mappings to determine the cause and extent of the event that buried our specimens?"

Palfrey nodded slightly. "I believe the event was a massive mud slide originating in the hills just to the east. Beyond the foothills are the rocky high elevations that are visible from up top."

"It must have been quite extensive to cover an area the size you showed me on the printouts." Moreland said.

Palfrey nodded again. "Indeed. I believe as the Antarctic continent moved south they eventually entered the turbulent seas south of the 40th parallel. I think its safe to say that area has probably always been prone to extreme weather. Once the Antarctic entered the far southern ocean intense storms became a more regular occurrence here. I would guess an extended period of precipitation inundated this loose sandy soil on the slopes east of here and, suddenly, in a moment, it all let loose."

"They aren't buried very deep though." Moreland commented.

"I suspect we are out at the very fringe of the landslide. The volume of material was rapidly thinning." Palfrey said.

Moreland nodded. "I understand that. What I meant was, the shallowness of the muddy sand that covered these specimens we are seeing...I don't know. Seems like most of them could have just shook it off and moved on."

Palfrey nodded solemnly. "I have wondered about that myself. That is something of mystery."

"Well, it will be interesting the variety of species we find here." Moreland said.

"Yes, there's truly no telling how many species we may find here." Palfrey agreed.

"If we can sort out the mess." Moreland said.

"Yes, well, that might be a bit of a task." Palfrey conceded.

3

The next day found Moreland, Jessica and Palfrey out at the site working diligently in their respective areas. As usual, the fog quietly, sluggishly moved all around them.

They worked quietly for a little while. It seemed like a they were the only things in their own private universe. The only real exception was an occasional sound from somewhere in the distance. Moreland had assumed it was activity from the camp.

"Ugh." Jessica muttered with a shiver. "You're not in Montana now girl."

Moreland glanced over at Jessica and smiled. "Montana? No, Montana gets pretty hot in the summer. You were out there last year on Dr. Medford's dig, weren't you?"

Jessica nodded. "Yeah. And I'll take that heat any day. I don't like being cold."

"Medford? That buffoon. He loves publicity too much." Palfrey said with a dismissive wave.

"Well, he did—-" Before Moreland could finish her sentence a loud cracking sound shook the ground around them. It seemed to come from some where over their heads.

Moreland and Jessica both let out gasps. Palfrey hesitated for a moment as if he was listening for something else and then continued his work.

"What the hell was that?" Jessica asked.

"Just the ice." Palfrey said.

"Like the ice looming up over us?" Moreland asked.

Palfrey glanced over at her. "The ice is constantly shifting. Sometimes the cracks in the ice sheet end here in our trench."

"Oh, man, I thought the ice was going to come crashing down on our heads." Jessica said.

"Well, sometimes chunks of the ice do come down." Palfrey said still working.

"Uh...so, like that might have crushed us?" Jessica asked. She looked over at Moreland.

Palfrey stopped his careful digging. "Oh, I doubt it. We're not that close to the ice wall here."

"OK, well, that's good to hear." Jessica said.

Palfrey glanced over in the direction the cracking had come from. There was nothing to be seen except fog.

"At least, I'm pretty sure we are." Palfrey said and then went back to digging.

"OK...and that's not good to hear." Jessica said. She and Moreland exchanged a look.

A short time later there was a trudging sound moving closer. Moreland and Jessica scanned around their foggy landscape trying to zero in on whatever was making the sound. Palfrey ignored the sound.

A moment later Private Devon emerged from the gray mist carrying a small thermal bag. He stopped between the area where Moreland knelt and the spot Jessica sat.

Devon smiled at them and began unzipping the thermal bag. "Thought you guys might enjoy a little hot chocolate."

"Oh my God." Jessica said hopping up and walking over to him. "You're a godsend."

"Can't argue with that." Moreland said as she made her way over to Devon. "You're...Private Devon, right?"

Devon nodded. "Scotty, ma'am."

"Thank you, Scotty." Jessica said accepting the cup handed her.

"Yes, thank you." Moreland said. Her eyes met Devon's and she glanced towards Palfrey.

Devon shook his head. "He never takes anything."

Moreland nodded. "Some things never change."

Jessica took a sip of the hot chocolate. "Ah, something warm. I'm not sure if I should drink this or just pour it down my shirt. Well, if it wouldn't burn my boobs."

"I'm sure Private, I mean, Scotty, doesn't need to hear that." Moreland said.

"No problem ma'am. I'm in the Army. There ain't nothing anybody can say that hasn't been talked about in the barracks. Pour away." Devon said. He smiled at Jessica.

Jessica laughed and waved the cup towards the front of her coat as if she was about to oblige Devon.

When they finished their hot chocolate Devon retrieved the cups, repacked the thermal bag and disappeared back into the fog.

The afternoon wore on. Their progress was slow, but steady. Each of them had made headway at better defining the fossils in their respective areas.

"Oh. What's this?" Jessica said. She shifted her position so she could get a better angle to work the thing out of the soil.

Moreland turned to look at Jessica. "Found something?"

"Not sure. I think so. Yeah. Looks different than the other bones." Jessica said sliding something out of the ground and lifting it up to better look at it.

Moreland moved over next to Jessica. She stared at the object in Jessica's hands. Jessica handed it to Moreland.

"Its a piece of wood. Probably a fossilized section of a conifer. Nice. Bag it." Moreland said handing it back to Jessica.

Jessica studied the fossil for a moment. "Just a chunk of tree."

"Old tree." Moreland said with a smile as she went back to work.

Palfrey made a sound and Moreland looked over at him. He was standing a couple of steps back from his area staring at it.

"Something wrong?" Moreland asked.

Palfrey didn't look at her. He continued to stare at what he had uncovered. "The concentration."

Moreland got up and walked over to him. "The concentration?"

Palfrey waved a finger at what he had been working on. "There is a high concentration of fossils here."

Moreland nodded. "We knew that."

Palfrey sighed. "Yes, but they are oddly intact. I have seen nest locations and kill zones where extensive predation has taken place, but the fossils are all a jumble. The prey consumed piecemeal and the bones dropped all about. These appear to be nearly completely skeletons."

Moreland stepped to her left and studied Palfrey's excavation. "Definitely. This almost seems more like a fresco. There are multiple specimens here."

Moreland knelt down and ran her fingers along a fossil. "Interesting. They're twisted around a little, but these are tarsals."

Jessica joined the other two. "You know I found a chunk of a tree, right?"

Palfrey ignored her. "Indeed. I think that looks like pamprodactyly to me—-just turned and collapsed."

"Yeah. I was going to say that." Jessica said, a hint of sarcasm in her voice.

Moreland looked up at her and smiled. "Does somebody need a refresher on bone structures? Four toes. Three larger and one smaller and higher up."

"Right." Jessica said.

Moreland looked over at Palfrey. "Trinisaura. Or...maybe Morrosaurus."

Palfrey nodded. "Morrosaurus. The femur and tibia match very closely to what Novas found on Snow Hill."

"We've never seen this much of one before." Moreland said.

Palfrey thought for a moment. "Not of the Morrosaurus, no. This is truly excellent. But...these are powerful runners."

Moreland stood up. She stared down at the fossils for a moment. "Oh. The depth of the overburden."

"Yes." Palfrey said nodding slowly.

"Are you guys having a secret conversation here or what?" Jessica asked.

Moreland looked at Jessica. "Morrosaurus was a very capable runner. Probably faster than most of other species in this region. They were about five feet tall and maybe 15 feet long. And yet, they seem to have been buried by a sand and mud mixture about 18 inches deep."

Jessica shrugged. "Maybe they were caught off guard and they just choked on the mud. People can drown in two inches of water."

Moreland waved a hand back towards what was appearing to be a mass grave. "All of them?"

Jessica stared the fossils. "Hmm, does seem a little odd. One big massive grave site."

Palfrey and Moreland looked at each other.

"So...", Moreland said, "they were dead when the mud flow swept through."

Palfrey sighed. "But no predation. The bone structure is intact."

"What would kill so many in such a short period time of time?" Moreland asked. The question seemed to be directed more to herself than Palfrey.

They stood there quiet for a minute.

Moreland glanced over at Palfrey. "Subterranean gases?"

Palfrey shook his head slightly. He looked skeptical. "No indications of any significant volcanism in this area. I don't know. Very strange."

"Maybe they just got sick of the crappy weather here and started killing each other." Jessica said.

Moreland and Palfrey looked at Jessica.

Moreland couldn't tell if Jessica was serious or not. "That seems highly unlikely."

"Indeed." Palfrey said.

As the dim light of the evening slowly filled their foggy world Moreland, Jessica and Palfrey sat at a table in the dining tent. Beecham crossed the room with his own tray and sat down with them.

"Evening folks. How goes the digging?" Beecham's smile was friendly, but seemed a bit strained.

"Fine." Palfrey said staring down at his food.

Beecham gave Moreland a questioning glance.

"We are making great progress on uncovering fossils." Moreland said.

Beecham nodded slightly. "That would explain Dr. Palfrey's unbridled enthusiasm."

Moreland smiled. She always appreciated sarcasm. "We...are wrestling with something of a mystery."

"Really." Beecham said.

"We seem to have too many fossils in one general location. Doesn't make sense." Moreland explained.

Beecham gave a short laugh. He shook his head. "Scientists are the only people that get stressed when they find an abundance of exactly what they are looking for."

Moreland smiled. "I suppose so."

Beecham's humor faded. "Speaking of mysteries. I wanted to give you a heads up on something. The lift is temporarily shut down."

"Shut down?" Jessica stopped with her fork half to her mouth.

Beecham held up a hand. "Its not a big deal. It happens sometimes if the weather up top is really bad or they need to do some maintenance on the equipment. It shouldn't affect us at all."

"They didn't tell you why?" Moreland asked.

"I didn't talk to them as yet. I just got the message a little while ago from the communications guy. I'll find out what's going on and let you know." Beecham said.

4

The following morning Moreland sat across from Palfrey at breakfast. Palfrey had very little on his tray. He sat drinking his coffee.

"Are you feeling OK?" Moreland asked.

"Hmm, mm" Jessica said with a mouthful of scrambled eggs. She looked up and saw that Moreland was talking to Palfrey. She shrugged and kept eating.

"I'm fine." Palfrey said a slightly hoarse voice.

Ten minutes later they were walking the path out towards the dig site. It was obvious to Moreland that Palfrey was moving a little slower than normal, but she knew from experience there was no point in pressing him about how he was feeling. Short of death there was little that would keep him from coming out to the site.

They worked through the morning and stopped when Devon brought them a nice picnic lunch. Moreland noted that Palfrey seemed to still lack much an appetite.

Jessica gave Devon an appreciative smile. Moreland noticed Devon smiling back. She shook her slightly. That could be trouble, she thought.

"That is very kind of you." Moreland told Devon.

Devon smiled. "Digging is hard work."

"Yeah and lunch is the most important meal of the day." Jessica said.

"I thought that was breakfast." Moreland said.

"Yeah. That one too. All the meals are important." Jessica said biting into a sandwich.

Palfrey refused any food and continued working in his designated area.

When Moreland and Jessica had finished eating Devon collected the remains of the lunch and with a smile at Jessica he disappeared into the fog.

Again a quiet settled around them as they went back to their digging. Only the distant sounds of ice cracking could be heard. The isolation of the fog seemed to draw them into their own separate worlds.

Into the afternoon the work continued. Moreland sat back from her work. She rubbed her lower back. Too much leaning over the fossils. She glanced over at Palfrey as he grunted. He was staring at something very closely.

Moreland got up and walked over to Palfrey. She squatted down next to where he knelt over a fossil. He looked over at her. He waved towards the fossil he had been looking at.

"Look at this." Palfrey said.

Moreland leaned closer and stared at the exposed fossil. "A tibia. With some damage to it."

Palfrey nodded. "Yes. The damage."

Moreland glanced at Palfrey and then back at the fossil. She got a little closer. After a minute she sat back up.

Moreland hesitated. "I have seen a couple of marks similar to this over there." She pointed towards her area.

"I...thought they may have been the result of the debris flow damaging the bones, but..." Moreland said.

"But they are not random damage from aggregate in the debris." Palfrey said looking at Moreland.

"Claws?" Moreland ventured a guess.

Palfrey nodded slightly. "That's what it looks like. We can determine better after it's been scanned, but it appears to be damage from a claw."

Moreland looked puzzled. "That brings us back to predation. But...that doesn't make sense. Based on the small percentage of the whole fossil bed that we have exposed so far and the number of those showing this kind of damage...that would suggest..."

Palfrey nodded. "Yes. That a very large number of these animals were at least involved at some point in what looks to be some very violent life and death behavior."

Moreland shook her head slowly. "What could have killed so many of these Morrosaurus in this one location. The Morrosaurus were fast. They could outrun most anything that was big enough to hunt them. Were they trapped?"

Palfrey shook his head. "I don't know. We are getting more questions than answers."

Moreland stared back down at the fossil. "Whatever was capable of killing so many Morrosaurus in one location enmasse is not something we've seen before. I wonder what that thing looks like."

Again Palfrey shook his head. "Perhaps we will find it buried here too, somewhere."

"So, something cracked those bones before they were buried?" Jessica asked. She had come up behind Moreland and Palfrey while they were talking.

Moreland nodded. "Looks that way."

"Ah, good." Jessica said with a sigh. "I thought it was me. Thought I was hitting them too hard."

Moreland turned to look at Jessica. "Maybe you should show me your work. Just because, well, for the record, 'hitting them' is not a term used on paleontological dig sites."

"Still..." Palfrey said. "...considering the number of clusters of what appears to be fossils...this cannot be the work of a single predator."

Jessica shrugged. "Maybe they were starving and started killing each other."

Palfrey looked at Jessica and then at Moreland who sighed and shook her head with a slight shrug.

"Morrosaurus was an herbivore. They would not be killing each other." Moreland said to Jessica.

Moreland glanced over at Palfrey. She could tell that his breathing seemed a somewhat heavy and his shoulders sagged a little.

"Laurence, are you OK?" Moreland asked.

"What?" Palfrey turned enough to look at Moreland.

She could see his face looked flushed. "Are you feeling OK?"

Palfrey waved a dismissive hand towards her. "Fine. Fine."

"Perhaps we could call this good for today." Moreland said. "We don't need to dig up all the fossils in one day."

"I don't think that's even...oh, wait, that was sarcasm again wasn't it." Jessica said.

Moreland turned to give Jessica a quick stare.

Palfrey sighed. "I suppose. If you need to stop."

The fact that Palfrey agreed to stop before full darkness had set in confirmed to Moreland that he wasn't feeling 100%.

They packed their equipment back into the locker and headed back towards camp. It was a quiet walk back to the camp. As they made their way up through the central walkway of the camp they encountered Beecham. He had been walking in the opposite direction and would have walked right past them. He was clearly distracted.

"Is anything wrong?" Moreland asked.

Beecham gave a slight shrug. "Nothing really I guess. One of the soldiers that was sick, well, we sent him back up a few days ago."

"Was he that sick? I thought it was just some cold going around." Moreland said.

"He became feverish and...well, we had to restrain him." Beecham said.

"Restrain him?" Jessica asked.

Beecham nodded. "Like I said he was feverish. We were afraid he was going hurt himself. Anyway, they have better medical facilities up top than we do."

"Seems like a strong reaction to a cold." Moreland said.

"That's what our medic said too." Beecham said. "Still, we got word that he died."

"Oh." Moreland said.

Palfrey started coughing. Everyone looked at him. He waved them off.

"Just an allergy." Palfrey said between coughs. "Its this damned dusty soil."

"Well, we were just heading over to the dining tent do you want to join us?" Moreland asked Beecham.

Beecham gave a quick nod. "Sure. I could eat."

"Me too." Jessica said.

"That goes without saying." Moreland said glancing at Jessica.

"Right." Jessica started to laugh and then stopped. "Wait, what are you saying?"

"Not for me." Palfrey said. "I think I will skip dinner. I am going to lay down for a little while."

Palfrey turned and headed off in the direction of his tent.

Moreland watched with a concerned look on her face. A moment later he was just a vague form in the fog.

A short time later Beecham joined Moreland and Jessica at a table in the dining tent.

"So the medic had no idea why your sick soldier was so feverish?" Moreland asked.

Beecham shook his head. "No. He was one of the early crew members helping to get the camp initially set up. Maybe it's just from being down here in this dark dusty cold for too long."

"Has anyone else gotten that sick before now?" Moreland asked.

"No. Not really, I mean, we seem to have that perpetual cold going around, but other than that, well, there was the dog, I guess." Beecham said.

"Dog?" Jessica asked.

Beecham nodded. "Yeah. One of the soldiers somehow got permission to bring down a dog. Maybe they labeled it as a service dog. I don't know. It was a nice dog. Rex. That was his name. He was very popular. Retriever. Very friendly to everyone. He was here a couple of weeks, then, I don't know, something changed. Don't know. Maybe it was just this place."

"What do you mean he changed?" Moreland asked.

Beecham shrugged. "He...just seemed to get moody and then eventually he started growling and snapping at people. Then one night he even attacked the soldier that brought him down here. He ended up having to be put down."

"That's sad." Jessica said.

Beecham sighed. "Yeah, but it was against regulations that he was here anyway. So, there wasn't much latitude in how that was handled."

"Did they perform an autopsy on him?" Moreland asked.

Beecham looked at her oddly. "Uh, no. It was just a dog that very likely got distemper or something like that."

5

As Moreland and Jessica walked into the dining tent the following morning they spotted Palfrey sitting at a table sipping coffee.

"Are you feeling better this morning?" Moreland asked as they stopped by Palfrey's table.

He nodded. "I believe I do."

Moreland wasn't sure how much better he was. She thought he still looked pale, well, paler than usual for an old man.

Beecham came into the dining tent. He got himself a cup of coffee and sat down next to Moreland.

"You look like you had crappy night of sleep." Moreland said studying Beecham.

Beecham shrugged slightly. "Sleep can sometimes be hard to get."

Moreland watched Beecham for a minute. "But...that's not all that's bothering you."

Beecham sighed heavily. "The lift is still shut down. Word came down it's because they are on lock down up top."

"What does that mean?" Jessica asked.

"It means that everyone is confined to their tents unless they are on duty." Beecham said.

"Why?" Moreland asked.

Palfrey seemed to be ignoring the conversation.

"Uh, well, it seems they have had a murder up top. They are in the midst of investigating it." Beecham said.

"A murder?" Moreland asked.

Beecham nodded. "Yeah. It...can happen sometimes in places like this. Conditions are hard. People get isolated and depressed. Makes people do things they normally wouldn't."

"Damn." Jessica said quietly.

As Moreland, Jessica and Palfrey made their way out to the dig site, once again Palfrey seemed to lag a little behind the other two.

Moreland had slowed up a couple of times to let him catch up so they didn't lose sight of him in the fog.

They made good progress on exposing more fossils. At times, Moreland thought, it was almost crazy how as they worked to reveal one fossil another one emerged. In addition, many of them seemed to be nearly complete specimens.

"Are you on strike?" Jessica asked, looking at Moreland.

"Huh? Strike?" Moreland asked turning to look at Jessica.

"You're just sitting there staring at the ground." Jessica said.

Moreland sighed and looked back at her work. "I don't know. Not sure what it is I'm seeing."

Jessica came over and looked over Moreland's shoulder. "Wow. That's almost two complete skeletons."

"Yes." Moreland said studying the fossils.

"They almost look like..." Jessica started to say.

"Yeah." Moreland said. "Laurence, could you come here?"

Palfrey came over to them.

"What do make of this?" Moreland asked.

Palfrey studied the two skeletons for a moment. "Interesting. Well, if they were buried suddenly by rocks and debris we can expect to see a wide variation in poses."

"I suppose." Moreland said. "But these do appear to be engaged in something."

"Like...that one was biting the other one?" Jessica asked.

"Yeah. Kind of looks that way." Moreland said.

"Well, we can't jump to conclusions." Palfrey said. "As I said, these poses can be deceptive given the chaos of their terminal event."

"Yeah. Kind of like what I'm working on. A foot inside a rib." Jessica said.

"Really? Show me." Moreland said.

They moved to where Jessica worked. She pointed. "Right there. The toes of somebody are going right through someone else's rib cage."

They stared at it for a minute before Moreland turned to Palfrey.

"Kind of an odd coincidence. To find, in our first couple of specimens, that much engagement." Moreland said.

"Maybe." Palfrey gave a slight shrug. He was about to say more when he started coughing roughly.

Moreland had been watching him somewhat throughout the day. "We are making great progress. There's no hurry. Let's stop for today." Moreland rested a hand on Palfrey's shoulder.

Palfrey nodded and they packed up for the day. As they walked back into camp Moreland again put her hand on Palfrey's shoulder.

"You need to go have the medic check you out." Moreland told Palfrey.

Palfrey's tired eyes looked at Moreland and hesitated and then he nodded. Moreland knew that if he didn't object he must have not been feeling good at all.

The three of them started towards the Admin tent. From somewhere they heard what at first seemed like ice cracking, but somehow different. All three stopped for a moment and listened. The sound repeated. Definitely a banging sound. Different from the ice cracking.

"What's that?" Jessica asked.

Palfrey shook his head.

"Don't know." Moreland said.

"Sounded kind of like gunfire." Jessica said.

"Not sure." Moreland said.

"And...it sounded like it came from...above us." Jessica said. "Didn't it?"

"Maybe." Moreland said, clearly unsure.

They walked on to the Admin tent. When the entered the tent they saw Beecham sitting at his desk—-which was really just a folding table. He seemed stressed. In addition, despite the cold air he appeared to be sweating a little.

"I think the medic needs to take a look at Laurence." Moreland said.

Beecham opened his mouth to say something, but hesitated.

"Uh, yeah, that might be a problem." Beecham said.

"Why?" Moreland asked.

"We sent that sick soldier up on the lift the other day and the medic went with him. And...well, the medic hasn't come back down and..." Beecham stopped.

"OK. When is the medic coming back down?" Moreland asked.

"Yeah, that's the problem. They're telling us, you know up top, they're telling us, because of the murder investigation, at the moment, no one can go up or down on the lift. So the medic isn't coming back down." Beecham said. Beecham sighed and wiped a hand across his face. He glanced at his hand. He seemed to be surprised to see sheen of sweat on his palm.

"Well, get them back on the radio and let them know we have another sick person down here." Moreland said.

"I tried, but they don't seem to be answering the radio." Beecham said.

"Not answering the radio? That's ridiculous." Moreland said. She wanted to say more, but she was, for the moment, at a loss for words.

Out of the corner of her eye Moreland noticed Palfrey wobbling a little.

"We need to get Laurence on to a cot." Moreland said and with Jessica's help they moved further into the Admin tent and to a cot. They laid him down and he closed his eyes dropping off to sleep.

After a quick dinner Moreland and Jessica were back in their tent. Jessica lay back on her cot resting. She peeked over at Moreland and saw her just sitting on the edge of her cot staring into space.

"Worried about the Dr. Palfrey?" Jessica asked.

"A little, I guess." Moreland answered.

"Something else bugging you?" Jessica asked.

"I don't know. Just an odd feeling." Moreland said.

"Like?" Jessica asked.

Moreland shrugged. "I don't know. Nothing, I guess." Moreland stretched her stiff back.

Shortly after the light went out both of them fell asleep to the steady hum of the generators.

"What the hell was that?" Moreland sat up on her cot.

"What? What are you talking about?" Jessica slowly sat up. "Wait, I think I heard something. I mean, I think something woke me up. Maybe I was dreaming it."

"No." Moreland said. "You weren't dreaming it. That was a gun shot."

Moreland got up and went to the opening of the tent. She peeked out, but through the darkness and the fog she didn't see anything stirring.

"What is it? What do you see?" Jessica asked.

Moreland shook her head and slowly let the tent flap close again. She turned back to her cot.

"Nothing." Moreland said. "I didn't see anything."

They both laid back down. Jessica was back to sleep within minutes. Moreland laid awake for awhile before restless sleep finally came to her.

In the morning, after a brief and quiet breakfast, Moreland and Jessica stopped by the Admin tent. Moreland wanted to check on Palfrey. She also wanted to ask Beecham about the gun shot during the night.

They walked into the front part of the large tent, but Beecham, nor anyone else, was around. They moved on further back and into the area used as a temporary medical facility. There were two people laying on cots, but no one attending them. Moreland and Jessica went to Palfrey's bedside.

Palfrey looked pale. He was asleep. They waited for a couple of minutes and then decided to head out to the dig site.

They walked in silence for most of the way to the dig site. It seemed that this morning the fog was little lighter. As they drew near the excavation Jessica stopped and turned to look at Moreland.

"Things aren't really going like they are supposed to, are they?" Jessica asked.

Moreland stopped, but did not look directly at Jessica. She seemed to just stare out into the fog.

"No. It has not, to say the least." Moreland said.

"Do you think we are in danger here?" Jessica asked.

Moreland sighed. "I don't know. I just don't know what's going on."

They both hesitated and then continued on to the site. As they reached the edge of the site it was Moreland that stopped. She had been staring straight ahead and as the site came into focus she stood looking at it. The lighter fog and the fact this spot was slightly higher than the surrounding area allowed them to view all three sections they had been working on.

"What?" Jessica asked stopping next to Moreland.

Moreland looked at the area she had been working in and then at Jessica's section before her eyes finally stopped at the fossils Palfrey had exposed.

Moreland didn't answer Jessica. She took several determined strides over to Palfrey's area. She stood staring at what he revealed.

Jessica joined her. "What are you looking at?"

Moreland pointed. "This."

Jessica stared at the fossils. "OK...he's cleared a pretty wide area already. Pretty good for an old man."

"I mean, well, what do you see?" Moreland asked.

"Uh," Jessica hesitated. It seemed like a trick question. Like she was supposed to see something amazing, but, honestly, she just saw a jumble of fossilized bones. "The bones of...one of those... Moronosauruses..."

"Morrosaurus." Moreland said. "And yes, but specifically what bones?"

Jessica studied the area for a moment. "Uh, looks like the ribs."

"Right. How many?" Moreland asked.

"How many ribs? I don't know. Do you know how many ribs one of these...Morbidsauruses are supposed to have?" Jessica asked.

"Morrosaurus. Do have some kind of mental block on the name of this dinosaur?" Moreland asked looking at Jessica.

Jessica shrugged. "Maybe. I might."

"How many rib cages?" Moreland asked.

"Oh, uh, two, I guess." Jessica said.

"So, two Morrosaurus here. Notice anything about both rib cages?" Moreland asked.

Jessica still thought there was some trick to the question, but she leaned a little closer.

"I don't know. Hard to tell. They're all busted up." Jessica said.

"Right." Moreland said.

Jessica didn't understand. Moreland seemed to imply she had just proven something, but Jessica didn't get what she was supposed to be seeing.

"Well, I guess, if its like Dr. Palfrey says, that the avalanche buried these creatures then I guess they would be broken up some." Jessica said.

Moreland shook her head. "I don't think that's what happened to these two. Look at this rib cage. The broken ribs are right along this line right here." Moreland pointed. "The whole rib cage isn't broken up—-just this area. As if something struck it right there and torn those ribs apart."

"Maybe something in the avalanche hit the animal in the ribs." Jessica offered.

"Maybe." Moreland said turning to the other rib cage. "But this one has the same injury."

Moreland looked at Jessica. "What do you think the odds are that two Morrosaurus both died from the same injury in the same spot?"

Jessica hesitated. "Oh, yeah. That does seem a little strange."

"Unless…" Moreland said, thinking out loud.

"Like they were fighting." Jessica blurted out.

Moreland glanced at her. "Well, yeah, basically, that's what I was wondering. But then the question is, if they were fighting among themselves, why?"

"Why does anyone kill anyone else? Its either money, love or sex." Jessica said.

"Well, I think we can rule out money and love." Moreland said. "Still, male animals don't generally fight to the death in trying to establish mating rights or in protecting their territory. Its not a practice that would make sense for long term species survival."

Jessica sighed. "I don't know. Maybe they all just went crazy."

Moreland shook her head. "Just doesn't make sense."

They pulled their tools out of the equipment locker and began working. They worked for a while in silence before Jessica finally spoke up.

"You know, its weird." Jessica said.

"What's weird?" Moreland said.

"Well, I know that Dr. Palfrey doesn't usually say much during the day out here, but it somehow seems even quieter without him." Jessica said.

Moreland glanced over at Palfrey's work area. "Yeah. It does."

"And I know he's just an old man, but, I don't know, I feel a little more vulnerable without him here." Jessica said.

"Well they say there is safety in numbers, but that actually stems from an inherent instinct within us. We genuinely feel safer when there's more of us around." Moreland said, still poking at the underside of a Morrosaurus jaw.

"Maybe." Jessica said. "But I've been to a couple of parties where that wasn't true."

There was a scuffle behind Jessica and she spun around with a reflexive scare. "Shit!"

Moreland looked over to see Devon walking up to Jessica.

"Damn, don't scare me like that." Jessica said.

"Sorry, Miss." Devon said.

"And don't keep calling me Miss. I told you the other day to call me Jessica." Jessica said firmly.

"Right. Sorry." Devon set his now well traveled thermal bag down.

Moreland stood up and walked over to them. She expected Devon to have found Jessica's scare to be humorous, but his face looked worried.

"Is everything OK?" Moreland asked Devon.

Devon was unzipping the bag. He stopped unzipping and hesitated. He looked up at Moreland.

"Not sure if I am supposed to be telling you about this, but...we found a body today." Devon said.

"A body?" Moreland asked.

"Like a dead body?" Jessica asked.

Moreland glanced over at Jessica. "You don't usually refer to a live person as 'a body.'"

Jessica ignored Moreland.

"Yeah." Devon said. "He was definitely dead."

"Well, don't just sit there. Tell us what happened." Jessica said anxiously.

"One of the other soldiers found the body not far from where the platform sits. It looks like he fell. From the top." Devon said.

"Fell? Has that ever happened before?" Moreland asked.

Devon shook his head. "No. Never."

"Maybe in this fog the guy just lost his way." Jessica suggested.

Devon shook his head skeptically. "I doubt it. The edge is clearly marked in both directions for almost a mile out and it was drilled into us to be careful up there. Besides, the fog is pretty much only down here."

"What do they want us to do with him?" Moreland asked.

"No one has told us anything." Devon said.

"They're still not letting anyone go up or down?" Moreland asked.

Devon shook his head.

"Damn, this place gets creepier and creepier every day." Jessica said.

They finished up their midday snack and Devon began packing up the thermal bag again.

Moreland glanced over at Jessica who was preoccupied jamming the last of her sandwich into her mouth.

"Scotty?" Moreland asked.

"Yes ma'am?" Devon answered.

"Do you have any pressing assignments you need to get done today?" Moreland asked.

Devon thought for just a moment. "No ma'am."

"Maybe you could just hang with us this afternoon." Moreland purposely did not frame it as a question.

Jessica looked up at Moreland and then over at Devon. She gave Devon a smile and a nod.

"Sure. I can stay." Devon replied.

Late in the afternoon Moreland decided they had done enough for the day. She was anxious to get back and check on Palfrey. The events of the last few days were starting to accumulate and she could not seem to shake a very unsettling feeling. She was determined, though, not to continue expressing it to Jessica. It was obvious that Jessica was feeling it too.

Moreland walked ahead of the other two on their way back to camp. Thoughts were spinning through her head. Behind her she could hear the quiet conversation between Devon and Jessica. Devon had spent the afternoon sitting near Jessica while she explained paleontological processes and theories to him. While Jessica's lecture may have been occasionally inaccurate, Moreland had said nothing. She had just smiled. Some things you just can't stop.

They walked into camp and Moreland headed straight for the Admin tent. She pulled the flap back and walked in. Beecham lifted his head up from his desk. His eyes looked weary and bloodshot.

"How is Dr. Palfrey?" Moreland asked.

Beecham rubbed a hand across his face. "Not much different I'm afraid. Still running a fever."

"What about this soldier that fell?" Moreland asked.

Beecham sighed. "I don't know. His body is in the back. He died on impact."

"What does Major Wilkins have to say about it?" Moreland asked.

Beecham shook his head. "They won't answer."

"God damn it. That's just bullshit. I don't care what issues they are having up there they need to talk to us." Moreland said, exasperated. "Someone needs to go up there and find out what the hell is going on. They need to know we need help here."

Beecham nodded. "I am going to find someone with ice climbing experience and—-"

"Ice climbing?" Jessica interrupted.

Beecham looked puzzled at the question. "Yes, ice climbing."

"I don't understand. Just take the damned lift thingy up." Jessica said.

"We can't operate the lift from down here." Devon explained.

"What? That's ridiculous. What if, oh, wait, the crane is up there." Moreland said.

Beecham nodded. "Right. There was never a scenario in the plan that no one up there would pull us out."

"So they're just going to leave us here?" Jessica's voice starting rising towards panic.

"No." Beecham said. "They won't leave us here. Whatever is going on up there they'll sort it out and get to us. I just want to send someone up to update on our situation and get an assessment on when we can expect some assistance."

"So, someone would have to ice climb all the way back up there?" Moreland asked.

Beecham nodded. "I'm afraid so. But, I'll find someone with experience and get them going."

Moreland sighed. "Fine. I guess. I'm going to check on Laurence."

Moreland walked into the back of the Admin tent. Jessica and Devon followed her. Palfrey was laying on his cot. He was clearly sweating. Moreland knelt next to him. He stared at her and gave a weak smile.

"How...how goes the dig?" Palfrey asked.

Moreland gave him a brief update on their progress and the odd scene that seemed to be emerging from the arrangement of the fossils. Palfrey listened. His brow furrowed as he thought about what Moreland was describing.

"Never seen anything like that before." Palfrey said quietly. "Not even in sites with multiple predators. Doesn't make sense."

"Is it possible that its a behavior that simply has not been depicted in any fossil site to date? Or maybe its a behavior that subsequent descendants evolved away from." Moreland speculated.

Palfrey shook his head slightly. "I don't know. I will need some time to think on that."

Palfrey closed his eyes and seemed to be slipping into sleep.

Moreland stood up. She looked past Palfrey's cot at another cot further into the tent. There was body there completely covered by a sheet. Next to that cot was another person resting on their own cot and sweating like Palfrey was.

Jessica and Devon followed Moreland's gaze.

"Can we get out of here?" Jessica asked.

"Sure." Moreland said and the three of them left the Admin tent.

6

The following morning Moreland, with Jessica right behind her, pulled the front of the tent back. They were going to get some breakfast and then check on Palfrey.

"What the...?" Moreland almost ran straight into a soldier standing in the opening. He stared at Moreland and didn't move.

"Can I help you?" Moreland asked.

"Sorry——" The soldier's voice was hoarse. He coughed a couple of times and then looked back at Moreland. "Sorry, ma'am no one is to leave their tents."

"How do we eat?" Jessica asked over Moreland's shoulder.

Moreland waved a hand over her shoulder dismissing Jessica's question. "Why? What's going on? Are we under some kind of quarantine?"

The soldier cleared his throat. "Don't know for sure ma'am. I...think it has something to do with the murder."

"What?" Moreland asked, shocked.

"Shit." Jessica said.

"What murder?" Moreland asked.

Over the soldier's shoulder Beecham appeared out of the fog. He veered over to their tent.

"Its alright soldier. These two can come out." Beecham said.

The soldier nodded and stepped back. He hesitated for a moment unsure if he should stay on guard and then realized the pointlessness of it and walked away.

"Someone's been murdered?" Moreland asked.

Beecham's face displayed a look of utter dismay. He almost seemed like he was in genuine shock.

Slowly Beecham nodded. "Dr. Palfrey."

"What? Oh my God." Moreland's voiced cracked. "Laurence? How...how can that be? No one...he was..."

"Who would kill Dr. Palfrey? He was such a nice old man." Jessica said.

"I...I don't know." Beecham said. "I can't understand it. It doesn't make any sense."

"What happened?" Moreland asked.

"I found him this morning. It...looks like his throat was cut." Beecham said.

"You need to call Major Wilkins—-oh shit. Are they still not answering?" Moreland asked.

Beecham nodded. "Still nothing. It doesn't make any sense."

Despite the fact that Beecham seemed to be a competent administrator, it was obvious that this was outside of his experience. Not only did he appear to have no idea what to do next, but the thin film of sweat on him indicated he was likely sick as well.

"What the hell? This isn't some kind of bureaucratic problem. This is murder. They have to help us." Moreland said.

"I know. I know." Beecham said. "But I don't know what to do."

"I thought you were going to get someone to climb up and get some help for us." Moreland said.

"I was, but...well, we have a lot of pretty sick people right now. And...the only qualified climber we have is too sick to go up." Beecham said.

"A lot? I only saw Laurence and one other person in the Admin tent." Moreland said.

Beecham nodded. "The number of sick people has jumped within the last couple of days and I knew I couldn't accommodate them all in the Admin tent so I ordered them quarantined in their own tents."

"There it is again." Jessica said.

Moreland and Beecham turned to look at her.

"What?" Moreland asked.

"Listen." Jessica said.

They stood quiet for a moment and then they heard it. A cracking or banging kind of sound. It was difficult to tell what direction it was coming from, but it seemed like it was from over their heads.

"Yeah. I heard it earlier too." Beecham's face was a picture of extreme stress. "I...think they are gun shots."

"Is someone attacking the camp up there?" Jessica asked.

They all exchanged a worried look.

"I don't know what the hell is going on." Moreland said. She stood for a moment and took a couple of deep breaths. She couldn't wrap her brain around the idea of Laurence being murder. Her mind, in some kind of defensive mechanism, was shutting out the thought at the moment. She could see Beecham was not in good shape. As a matter of fact he looked like he might collapse at any moment.

Moreland huffed. It felt as if the last couple of days she had been getting hit with one new twist after another and she was getting tired of it.

"OK." Moreland said taking Beecham by the arm. "Come with me. Jessica stick with us."

"There's a murderer somewhere out here wandering around in the fog. I ain't going anywhere by myself." Jessica said.

They started off in the direction of the Admin tent. They had only gone a short distance before Jessica spoke again.

"Hey, you think we could stop by the Dining tent real quick?" Jessica asked.

Moreland twisted around to look at Jessica. "Really? Right now?"

Jessica shrugged. "Sorry, but it is time for breakfast. And...well, stress makes me hungry."

"Everything makes you hungry." Moreland said. "We'll eat later."

They walked a little further before Moreland slowed up.

"I just realized I don't know what tent is yours." Moreland said to Beecham.

"Its right next to the Admin tent." Beecham said.

"Ah, I guess that makes sense." Moreland led Beecham to his tent and helped him lie down.

"But...we've got to do something." Beecham objected.

"You're in no shape to do anything right now. Stay here. I'll figure something out and let you know a plan—-when I figure one out." Moreland told him.

Beecham seemed too weak now to object further and laid back closing his eyes. Moreland and Jessica left Beecham's tent. Moreland led them into the Admin tent.

Jessica stopped in the front area of the tent. "I...I can't go in there."

Moreland looked back at her. "Its OK. I understand. Just wait here."

Before Moreland could turn away Devon appeared in the opening of the Admin tent.

"Ah, Scotty. Perfect timing. Could you escort Jessica to the Dining tent?" Moreland asked.

Devon seemed like he wanted to ask something. He looked around and didn't see Beecham. He looked straight at Moreland and clearly made a decision.

"Yes, ma'am. What about you?" Devon asked.

Moreland glanced at the canvas flap separating the front part of the Admin tent from the Medical area in the back and then back at Devon.

"I'll be OK. I...need to check something here." Moreland said.

Devon looked at Moreland. He clearly knew about Palfrey's murder. He gave short nod and put a hand on Jessica's back. The two of them left the Admin tent.

Moreland turned and hesitated in front of the opening to the Medical area. She was bracing herself for what she knew she would find there.

Slowly Moreland pulled the flap back. Her eyes fixed on Palfrey immediately. Her stomach churned and her chest felt tight. My God, she thought, there's a lot of blood.

It took her a long minute to realize that she wasn't moving at all. She was barely breathing. With all of the inner strength she could muster she pushed past the tent flap and into the Medical area. She took a couple of steps forward and stopped again. She took a deep breath and tried to just focus on the scene in front of her as objectively as she could.

Palfrey lay across the cot, but not as if he had been resting in bed. Most of his body was on the cot with the exception of his lower legs. They drooped over the side. His head, though, was at the foot of the cot. It looked more like he had been standing and simply fell back on to the cot.

There was a lot of blood. The top of his shirt around the neck and his left shoulder were soaked with blood. A streak of red ran down the length of his left arm as it dangled over the edge of the cot, fingers nearly touching the floor. There was a large pool of blood under the cot and spread out across the floor.

It was Palfrey's neck that Moreland did not want to look at, but kept glancing back at. The deep cut ran around almost half of his neck. The gaping section was dark red.

Moreland suddenly felt dizzy. For a moment she was sure she was going to faint. She was acquainted with animal physiology as part of trying the to understand species long since dead, but this was something completely different. She had never seen anything like this up close and, particularly in this case, very personal.

Moreland took several quick breaths and she stared down at her feet. It seemed to steady her.

"I am so, so sorry, Laurence." Moreland said quietly as she made herself to look up again.

With a bit of an effort she forced herself to work through what she was seeing logically. Palfrey must have been standing up when the killer, well, killed him. It was difficult to tell if he had tried to fight off his attacker. Palfrey was old and sick. He wouldn't have had much strength to protect himself.

With even more effort, Moreland took another couple of steps forward. She stopped and made herself stare for a painful minute at the wound. She didn't have medical training, but even she could tell that Palfrey's throat had been cut with something very sharp. Standing here in the Medical section of the tent the first thing that came to mind was a scalpel.

Moreland glanced around the room. Over to one side was the medical cabinet. The door was open and among the medicinal bottles and bandages could be seen a variety of basic medical tools. Moreland nodded. Well, that's probably where the murder weapon came from.

Moreland tried to think like a detective. She had always enjoyed reading mysteries and had often thought of herself in a way not unlike a detective in her work. She worked at trying unravel the mystery of the fossils she uncovered. Identify them and try to decipher how they lived.

Think, she thought to herself. She slowly scanned the area right around the body for something that might serve as a clue about who would have done this to Laurence. The neck had been sliced from one side to the other. Both carotid arteries were surely cut. The blood, soaking the sheet, the thin mattress and the large pool all around the legs at the foot of the cot was a testament to that.

To make that long of a cut Laurence could not have been able to move as his throat was opened up. That seemed odd to Moreland. Whoever killed him must have been strong. Another thought came to Moreland. All that blood. How did the murderer not get covered in blood? And...Moreland looked down at the floor...not leave bloody footprints?

There were no bloody footprints. None. But there was something in the pool of blood. It was a little hard to make out what it was at first. Moreland leaned out over the blood. There it was. A scalpel.

Moreland thought about trying to reach out and pick it up, but then decided that would be a mistake. It was undoubtedly the murder weapon and this was now a crime scene. She had watched enough TV and movies to know that you were not supposed to disturb a murder scene.

She stared at the scalpel for a moment. It was possible that the scalpel had the fingerprints of the killer on them and she desperately wanted to know who would have killed Laurence and why. The answer to that seemed to be potentially sitting right there. Maybe...

Moreland tried to think. Do fingerprints remain on an object that's soaking in blood? She didn't know. Besides that, she was not knowledgeable enough or equipped to get the prints off the scalpel. It was likely anyway that the killer was wearing latex gloves from the cabinet. If the person wasn't wearing gloves, hmm, that wasn't very comforting. A killer that didn't care if you found out who they were. That's an even scarier person.

Moreland straightened up. She didn't think she was going to be able to figure out anything just standing here. She looked one last time at Laurence. She wanted to cover him up with a sheet. It just seemed like the decent thing to do, but the thought of disturbing a crime scene came to mind again. She decided to do nothing.

She slowly turned around and walked out of the medical area. She walked staring down at the floor. Her knees felt like jelly. There was bit of dizziness that she couldn't shake. Somehow they needed to get some help from above. She felt like she should go to the communications tent and try again to get a hold of someone up top. As she got to the entrance to the Admin tent she nearly ran into someone coming in.

"Oh, sorry." Moreland said stepping back from the doorway. A young sweaty soldier stared back at her.

"Uh, ma'am, where's Mr. Beecham?" The soldier asked.

"Mr. Beecham is in his tent. He's sick." Moreland said.

The soldier just stood there. He was clearly unsure what to do.

"Is there something wrong?" Moreland asked.

The soldier hesitated. "Uh, Mr. Beecham told us to secure the camp, but, well, we don't know what we are securing it from or...what to do now."

Moreland sighed. She was a paleontologist, not an administrator or, for that matter, someone with extensive experience in crisis management.

"What is your name?" Moreland asked.

"Uh, Dylan ma'am. Corporal Dylan." Dylan told her.

"OK Corporal Dylan, I think Mr. Beecham was wanting the camp secured because so many people were getting sick and no one knows what it is from." Moreland said. She knew that wasn't exactly true, but it seemed like a reason that sounded good enough and not as likely to panic people than the fact that there was murderer running around the camp.

"OK, ma'am." Dylan stood looking at Moreland. Clearly he didn't know what he was supposed to do next or what he might tell the soldiers still actively on duty what they should be doing.

Moreland saw Dylan's hesitation. She didn't have an idea on what to tell the soldiers to be doing either, but before she could come up with something to tell the young man someone in the camp screamed. Both Moreland and Dylan stared out into the foggy air in the direction the scream came from.

Without really thinking Moreland took off towards where she thought the scream had come from. Dylan followed her at a run. They had covered about a third of the camp's length without seeing or hearing anything more when something to Moreland's right caught her eye.

Moreland slowed as she saw a soldier staggering out from between two tents. There was blood soaking the front of her shirt and pants. She took a couple more shaky steps and then fell to her knees. Moreland ran over to her and caught her just before she was going face plant into the dirt.

Moreland tilted the young black girl back a little to try to see where she was injured. Moreland's stomach turned a little at the amount of blood. It was a lot. Too much. It was quickly obvious there was nothing they could do for her.

"What happened? Who did this?" Moreland asked the girl.

The girl's eyes were open, but they were unfocused. Moreland could see the life dropping out of her. She eased the girl down to the ground.

"Is she dead?" Dylan asked from behind Moreland's right shoulder.

Moreland nodded. "Yeah."

A movement from between the tents where the girl had walked out of drew Moreland's attention. She looked up and saw another soldier standing a short distance away. He was holding a large bloody knife. Their eyes met. The soldier's expression changed from shock to panic. He dropped the knife, turned and started running.

"Get him!" Moreland yelled over her shoulder to Dylan.

Dylan hesitated for just a moment and then took off after the other soldier.

Moreland did a cursory glance at the wounds the young soldier laying in front of her had suffered. Moreland struggled as she did it. Despite not knowing this young girl at all it was just as difficult for her to try look at her nasty gaping wounds as it was to look at Palfrey.

Fighting off some dizziness Moreland thought she could make out about four deep stab wounds to the girl's abdomen. She stood back up on shaky legs. A short distance away she saw the knife laying on the ground. It occurred to Moreland that she should probably pick the knife up and store it somewhere. It was evidence in a homicide.

Moreland stepped over to the knife. She knew she shouldn't just pick it up and mess up the fingerprints on it. She glanced around. There wasn't anything here she could use to scoop the knife up. Before she could decide what to do she heard quick footsteps coming out of the fog behind her. She whirled around. Corporal Dylan.

"Shit." Moreland said quietly. Her hands were shaking a little. She looked at Dylan.

"Did you catch him?" Moreland asked.

Dylan shook his head. "No ma'am. Lost him in the fog."

"Damn." Moreland said. "So our killer is still out there somewhere."

"Well…" Dylan's voice trailed off.

"What? What's wrong?" Moreland asked, bracing for yet another ugly problem.

"Well, ma'am, I know him. Private Rico, I mean. And, well, he's a pretty good guy and all and, well, I just don't think he's a killer." Dylan said.

"He was standing near the body holding the bloody knife that killed," Moreland turned and pointed at the body, "her."

"I know." Dylan nodded slowly. "But, I don't know. It just don't make sense."

Moreland sighed. "OK. Well, find me something to pick up that knife so we can preserve the fingerprints on it."

Dylan glanced down at the knife. After a moment he pulled his right arm up into the sleeve of his shirt. With his hand inside the shirt sleeve he reached down and picked up the knife by the blade and held it up for Moreland to see.

Moreland looked at him for a moment and then nodded. "OK, well, better your shirt than mine."

Moreland turned and stepped over to the body. "We'll take the knife over to the Admin tent and then I need you to find a couple of other people to help get this body over to the Admin tent and…covered up."

"We're going to cover up what happened?" Dylan asked.

Moreland's brow furrowed. "No. Take the body over to the Admin tent, put it on a cot and cover it with a sheet."

"Oh, right. Yes ma'am." Dylan said looking a little relieved.

They walked back over to the Admin tent. Moreland knew they had to do something now. Right now. She left Dylan at the Admin tent to deal with the knife and the body. She turned and walked over to Beecham's tent.

At the entrance to Beecham's tent she called out to him. She thought she heard something, but wasn't sure what. She decided to just go in. She found Beecham still laying on his cot. He looked at her and managed a weak smile.

"How...how are things?" Beecham asked.

Moreland shook her head a little. "Not great. Another dead body. Its murder. I saw the guy who did it, but Corporal Dylan couldn't catch him. He said the soldier's name was Rico."

Beecham stared at her. "I know that boy. He's a good young man. That doesn't make sense."

Moreland shrugged. "That's what Dylan said. I don't know."

"Are you sure?" Beecham asked.

"Well, he was standing over the body with a bloody knife." Moreland said.

Beecham sighed. "I don't understand what's happening. Who was the victim?"

Moreland shook her head. "I don't know who the girl was. Dylan is getting the body moved into the Admin tent. How are you doing?"

Beecham made a feeble effort to shrug. "I don't know. Very weak. Doesn't feel like I am getting better. It's weird, though."

"Weird? What do you mean?" Moreland asked.

Beecham shook his slightly. "Not sure. Almost, at times, feels like, I don't know, in the background."

"In the background? What does that mean?" Moreland asked.

"I don't know. I guess like someone else is in the driver's seat." Beecham said. "Can't really explain it better."

"OK." Moreland patted Beecham's shoulder. "Get some rest. I will check back later on you."

Beecham nodded.

Moreland walked out of Beecham's tent. She stood for a moment, unsure what to do next. Finally, with a shake of her head, she started walking back towards the Admin tent. She needed to talk to Major Wilkins or someone up top. They had to answer them now.

Moreland ducked into the Admin tent and turning to the left went into a small area where a large radio sat on a folding table. She stopped when she entered through the flap that separated that area from the entry area of the Admin tent. She looked around the small area. No one.

"Great." Moreland said. "Where the hell is the communications guy?"

Moreland stepped over to the radio. She stared at it. She tried reading some of the labels on buttons, but most of them were just abbreviations. This radio set was sophisticated. It was clearly meant for more than just chatting with someone up the hill.

Twice she reached out to flip a switch and pulled her hand back. A mic sat straight in front of her, but she knew she would have to do something to make it live. In addition, she thought, this is the Army's radio. There was probably a bunch of protocol and secret codes or other such shit that she didn't know anything about. Even if she could get it to work without the right authorization codes or whatever, no one up top would probably talk to her.

Moreland stood with her hands on her hips and sighed.

"Hey."

Moreland jumped and spun around.

"Damn it, Jessica." Moreland said.

"What? I just said hey." Jessica said indignantly.

"Sorry. Its just...things are getting a little crazy around here." Moreland said.

"A little? Man, I've been hearing all kinds of sounds out there." Jessica asked. "People are getting all spooky and jittery."

"Yeah, well, there was another murder." Moreland said.

"What? Another one?" Genuine fear ran through Jessica's voice.

"Yeah." Moreland said. She felt a certain exhaustion creep over her. She knew it was the stress, the fear and the fact that she felt like she was trapped in this nightmare.

"I...I don't know what to do...I'm scared." Jessica stammered.

Moreland nodded slightly. "I know. We need to try to get a hold of someone up top again."

"Mr. Beecham said they won't answer." Jessica said.

"I know, but we need help. We need it now." Moreland said.

Jessica nodded. She looked at the radio equipment.

"You know how to operate this thing?" Jessica asked.

Moreland glanced at the radio. She shook her head. "No. Not really."

Jessica stepped a little closer and stared at the various buttons and dials. "Why the hell can't they just put a big fucking switch that says On and Off?"

Moreland shrugged. "I don't know. I guess because they're the Army."

"Are you people looking for the Army?"

Both Moreland and Jessica jumped and turned around.

"Damn it, Scotty." Jessica said. "You scared us to death."

Devon looked surprised. "Oh, sorry."

"Can you operate this?" Moreland waved towards the radio.

Devon stared at it for a moment. "Well, its been a little while since I had a brief instruction on these things, but, yeah, I think so."

Moreland stepped aside. "Please, try to get a hold of Major Wilkins. If anyone up there answers tell them that Dr. Moreland needs to talk to Major Wilkins immediately."

Devon sat down in the chair and studied the equipment for a minute. Slowly he started flipping several switches and talked into the mic calling to anyone above to answer them. He kept trying for several minutes with no answer.

Moreland started reaching out to put a hand on Devon's should and tell him to give up on it when a voice came over the speaker.

"Yeah, yeah, we're here. Don't know for how much longer. Main camp, can you hear us? For God's sake help us..." The voice stopped.

Devon tried to get them to respond again, but got nothing.

"Help them? We're the ones that need help and they expect us to go help them?" Jessica said.

Devon shook his head. "No. Not us. They were trying to call the Main camp."

"They were calling the Main camp for help?" Moreland asked.

"Sounds like it." Devon said looking up at Moreland standing next to him.

"Shit." Moreland said. "They're not going to be able to help us at all."

"Why? What's going on up there?" Jessica's voice was anxious.

Moreland shook her head. "I don't know, but we are truly on our own here."

7

The three of them walked out of the Admin tent. Moreland turned to her right. Jessica and Devon followed her.

"Where are we going?" Jessica asked.

"To see Beecham." Moreland answered.

They reached Beecham's tent and went in. Moreland walked over to Beecham's cot. He didn't look good.

"Beecham." Moreland said. "Randolph."

Beecham's eyes opened a little. He seemed to stare at Moreland for a moment before finally focusing enough to acknowledge her.

"Doctor." Beecham whispered.

"We tried the radio again. We heard someone, but they didn't seem to be speaking to us. They were calling for help from the Main camp." Moreland told Beecham.

Beecham shook his head a little. "That doesn't sound good."

Moreland nodded slightly. "No, it doesn't. Is there anyone else that could climb up and get us help?"

"Sorry." Beecham said very quietly. "Only found one person with ice climbing experience, but she was too sick to attempt it."

"Damn." Moreland said. She sat silently for a minute staring down at the floor. Finally she sighed.

"Do you have any of those ice gripping things? You know, the things that go on boots, oh, and the ice picking things?" Moreland asked.

Beecham looked Moreland. "You're going to climb up there?"

Moreland gave a small shrug. "I don't know, but someone is going to have to try."

Beecham nodded. "I guess so. Yeah, I think there are some in one of the main equipment lockers. Don't remember which one. They were there for emergency use so we've never pulled them out."

"Well, this seems kind of like an emergency to me." Moreland said. "And the main equipment lockers are...?"

"I know where they're at." Devon said.

"Good luck with..." Beecham's voice trailed off as his eyes closed.

They left Beecham in his tent softly wheezing.

Moreland looked at Devon. "Lead on."

The three of them walked down through the center of the camp. There was a strange mix of sounds coming from all around them. Some people were coughing harshly. There was the sound of people crying. In some tents it sounded as if someone was kicking everything in their tent all over the place. The sounds were unnerving. More so because the fog made it difficult to see anything more than wispy gray shapes moving just out of their clear vision.

As they made their way further Moreland stopped suddenly. Devon and Jessica had taken two steps more before realizing that Moreland had stopped. They turned to look back.

"What?" Jessica asked.

Moreland was squinting towards the front of a tent. She took a step in that direction.

"Corporal Dylan?" Moreland called out.

"Yes ma'am." Came a hoarse reply.

Moreland moved over to where Dylan was slouched against the front of a tent. He didn't look good.

"What happened?" Moreland asked.

"Oh, shit." Jessica's voice spit out before Dylan could answer.

Moreland turned and saw Devon and Jessica standing over the soldier murdered earlier. The one Dylan was supposed to be taking to the Admin tent. Moreland turned back to Dylan.

"What happened?" Moreland asked again.

"Sorry ma'am." Dylan said. His voice wavered a little. He was sweating heavily now. "I...I couldn't find anyone to help me and...and I tried moving..." He waved a hand towards the body.

"OK. OK, never mind about that right now. You need to get back to your tent." Moreland said.

Dylan managed to nod.

"OK, where's your tent?" Moreland asked.

Dylan lifted a hand up and his thumb indicated he was leaning on it.

"Ah, well that simplifies things a bit." Moreland said. She turned towards Devon. "Scotty, give me a hand."

Devon moved quickly to take the other side of Dylan and they moved him into his tent and down on to his cot.

"Needless to say, you need to stay here." Moreland said.

Dylan gave a weak nod.

Devon and Moreland walked out of Dylan's tent. They joined Jessica who had turned her back to the dead body.

"Can we just get out of here?" Jessica asked.

"Yeah..." Moreland started to say. "Wait. You notice something?"

"You mean besides the fact that we're just standing here next to another dead body?" Jessica grumbled.

"No. There's no hum." Moreland said.

Devon turned his head back in the direction of the Admin tent. "Yeah. The generators aren't running."

"Oh, yeah. I saw the lights go out a little while ago." Jessica said.

"You might have said something." Moreland said.

Jessica shrugged. "It wasn't a big deal. They don't do much good here anyway. They're just dim glowing things in the fog. Can we just find someone to climb up top and get us out of here?"

Moreland looked at Devon. "Are all the heaters in this place propane?"

Devon shook his head. "No. Some of them are electric. They depend on the generators. And so does a lot of the food."

Moreland's eyes met Devon's. She could tell the same thought was running through his head.

"Damn." Moreland said. "Where exactly are the generators at?"

Devon pointed back the way they had just come. "About 50 yards past the Admin tent."

"What? Why do you care where the generators are? They're not going to get us out of here." Jessica said.

Moreland turned to look at Jessica. "We can't leave these sick people down here without the generators. They would freeze or starve."

Jessica seemed like she was going to say something and then changed her mind.

Moreland turned now to Devon. "Know anything about running a generator?"

Devon shrugged. "I have had to help refuel them a couple of times. I don't think that exactly qualifies me as an expert."

"Actually, right now, it does." Moreland said. "Let's go."

The three of them turned and headed back towards the Admin tent. Devon led them past the Admin tent and beyond. There was another tent, larger than the usual ones. Devon hesitated as the drew near the larger tent.

"What's wrong?" Moreland asked.

Devon frowned. "There should a guard there." He pointed at the front of the large tent.

"Why? What's in it?" Jessica asked.

"That's the primary supply tent for the entire camp. Food and medical supplies and stuff like that." Devon said.

"Well, we can't worry about that right now." Moreland said.

They moved past the supply tent and past a couple of orange markers. At a red marker Devon veered right. A short distance further and they could make out the gray shapes of the two generators. Each one was about the size of a car.

Devon walked up to the first generator. He did a quick inspection.

"Huh. Looks like it has gas. That's odd." Devon said.

"What?" Moreland asked.

"Looks like someone just turned it off." Devon said.

"Why would someone do that? The camp depends on these to survive down here." Moreland said.

Devon shrugged. "Don't know."

"So, we can just turn it back on, can't we?" Moreland asked.

Devon ran a hand along the side of the generator. He wagged his head a little. "Its...not quite that simple."

"Can't anything down here be simple." Jessica said.

"These are diesel generators. They can be hard to start when they are cold. The fuel gets thick. Won't flow into the engine." Devon explained.

"Shit." Moreland said. "Well, how do they normally start a cold diesel engine?"

"Well," Devon said stepping around to the back side of the generator, "I think there's battery powered heater back here that's supposed to heat up the fuel. Here it is." He flipped a switch.

"Good." Moreland said. "Start it up and then we'll take look at the other one."

"Uh, well, its going to take some time for the heater to warm up the fuel enough to be able to start it up." Devon said.

Moreland sighed. "OK...so how long will it take to heat up the fuel?"

Devon shrugged. "Sorry. I don't really know. I know what the procedure is, but I never had to go through it before."

Moreland waved a hand in the air. "OK, to hell with this one, let's look at the other one."

They walked over to the second generator a few yards away. Devon looked that generator over.

"This one's out of gas. Odd that whoever was on the duty roster for the generators hasn't been out here." Devon said.

"They're probably sick like everyone else." Jessica said.

"Ah," Devon said with a nod, "probably so."

"So we just need to refuel this one?" Moreland asked.

"Yeah, as long as—-" Devon started to say.

"Jesus, what's that smell?" Jessica said raising a hand up to her nose.

There had been a slight change in the direction of the nearly nonexistent breeze and the smell hit all three of them.

"Oh, God." Moreland said also covering her nose.

Devon's brow furrowed. "That smells like fuel. Lots of it."

Devon glanced at the generators to orient himself and then turned to his left staring out into the gray fog.

"The fuel shed is that way." Devon pointed.

Devon started walking in the direction he had pointed. Reluctantly Moreland and Jessica followed. A bright red flag appeared ahead of them. They passed it and another one before they could make out small corrugated building——and something in front of the building.

They drew closer and Devon stopped. Moreland and Jessica were a couple of steps behind him. A short distance ahead was a man standing motionless. He appeared to be soaking wet which meant that, if he had been that way for very long, he must be freezing.

"Simmons?" Devon asked.

The ground all around Simmons and the small building was wet.

Simmons made a sound. It seemed to be somewhere between an articulated word and a growl.

"Oh shit. That's the fuel." Moreland said. "He's covered in it."

"Simmons, what are you doing?" Devon asked. Devon started to take a step forward, but just as he did Simmons lit a lighter. He just held it in his hand and stared at it.

Moreland grabbed the back of Devon's coat and pulled him back a step.

"Oh, Jesus, no..." Jessica whimpered.

"Back up." Moreland said.

Before anyone could move Simmons touched the lighter to his chest. His body exploded into flame. The ground all around him was engulfed in fire. The fire shot back to the shed and a moment later explosions started firing off in rapid succession.

Moreland, Devon and Jessica all stumbled backwards and fell down. There was a rush of intense heat rolling over them. All three scrambled backwards a dozen yards. They could still see Simmons. Strangely he was still standing. Moments later, though, his body fell like a small tree slamming down to the ground.

8

Moreland looked over at Devon as the three of them leaned up against the generator. Behind them, on the other side of the generator the fuel shed was still blazing away.

"Can you start the one generator now?" Moreland asked panting slightly from the blast and then scrambling back to the generators.

Devon nodded. "I can. I don't think there was a lot of fuel left in that one, though. Won't last too long."

"I don't understand. Why would he do that?" Jessica asked. She started crying and leaned into Devon. Devon put an arm around her.

"I don't know." Devon said. "Simmons had been in the Army a long time. People looked up to him."

"Let's get this one generator started." Moreland said.

"OK." Devon walked to the other generator. It took him a few minutes before the generator sputtered to life.

"Let's get back to camp." Moreland said.

On the walk back to camp Jessica clung to Devon's arm.

As they drew near the back of the Admin tent Devon stopped. Jessica had been staring down at the ground. She seemed to not want to see anything more. She didn't even look up when Devon stopped.

Moreland too had been watching the ground in front of her feet. Her mind was just spinning. Their options were not good and she knew it. She nearly walked into Devon's back.

"What?" Moreland asked.

Devon was staring into the fog to his right. "Not sure." He pointed to their right.

It took Moreland a moment to see it. A dark streak on the gray and sandy ground.

They moved closer and Moreland knelt down for a closer look.

"Shit." Moreland said. She stood up. "It's blood."

Moreland looked to the left and could just make out the back of a tent. The tent looked a little odd. It took her a moment to realize the back of the tent appeared to be sliced open.

"What tent is that?" Moreland asked.

Devon stared for a moment. He pointed to another tent. "That's the Admin tent."

"Then...shit. That's Beecham's tent." Moreland said. She turned to see the blood trail led off into the fog away from the torn tent.

"You think...maybe the murderer...?" Devon hesitated.

"Killed Beecham?" Moreland asked. "God I hope not, but if he did," Moreland turned to look at the blood trail, "we should try to catch up with him before he gets away again."

"You want to chase after some crazy guy who's going around stabbing people?" Jessica asked. Her voice was almost hoarse with fear.

"Him?" Devon asked. "You still think Rico is the murderer?"

Moreland looked at Jessica and then Devon. "Yes. And yes. Look, we need to try to stop this madness."

"So we're just going to run after this crazed killer and then do what if we catch up to him? Throw rocks at him." Jessica kicked at the ground.

Moreland turned to look at Devon's waist. "You don't carry any weapons?"

Devon shook his head. "No ma'am. No one was expecting fossils to be dangerous."

Moreland sighed. She stood for a moment. She shook her head. "At this point, I don't care. I need to know what's happening."

Moreland turned and started walking away from the tents following the blood trail.

"Ma'am..." Devon started to say. "Damn it."

Taking Jessica by the arm Devon started after Moreland.

"Wait," Jessica started, "can't we just..."

"We can't let her walk out there alone." Devon said.

Jessica moaned a little, but kept pace with Devon. She sure as hell knew she didn't want to stand out here by herself.

A short distance further Moreland slowed. She stop for just a moment stepping over something.

When Devon and Jessica passed the spot they saw a bloody knife laying on the ground.

They continued on, but their trek didn't take them much further. A shape on the ground slowly materialized out of the fog ahead of them. Another few steps and it became clear it was a body. They stopped when they reached it.

"Beecham." Moreland said quietly.

Beecham's body lay on its side. He wasn't wearing a coat and his pallor was pale white. He was dead and there seemed to be a deep and nasty gash in his upper ribs. Somewhere in the vicinity of his liver.

"Can we go back now?" Jessica asked in a small voice.

Moreland gave a quick nod, turned and started walking back towards the camp. Devon and Jessica followed. They walked along the trail of blood. It was a sad and depressing guide back to Beecham's tent.

Moreland stared at the long gaping slash that had been cut vertically in the tent canvas.

"So...someone just cut their way into his tent and stabbed him?" Jessica said staring at the tent.

"I guess." Moreland said. Her voice betrayed some of the exhaustion that was overtaking her. "I just don't understand it. Someone is going around killing people, but...why?"

"Ma'am?" Devon asked.

Moreland turned to look at Devon. "Yeah, Scotty?"

"I think I should break into the weapons locker. I don't think it's safe here." Devon said.

"Oh, hell yes." Jessica said. "I would like a gun right now."

Moreland looked at Jessica. "Have you ever fired a gun before?"

Jessica hesitated. "No. But I would feel a lot better if I had one."

"You would be the only one." Moreland said.

"I'll shoot the first—-wait, was that sarcasm?" Jessica asked.

Moreland looked at Devon. "Where's the weapons locker?"

Devon pointed off into the fog. "That way."

"Lead on." Moreland said.

"First we need something to break the lock on the door of the locker." Devon said. He started walking around towards the front of Beecham's tent. Moreland and Jessica followed.

They walked a short distance down along the center of the camp. Devon stopped. He stood glancing in several directions.

"What's wrong?" Moreland asked.

"I was—-" It was all Devon got out before someone screamed from behind them. They turned to see a soldier sprinting out from between two tents with an ax raised up over his head. He was running straight at them.

Jessica screamed too, but she just stood there watching the guy closing in. Devon moved. He ducked to his right, hunched over and then threw himself into the soldier's mid section. His shoulder collided with the guy's ribs. The soldier buckled forward, still holding the ax, and then flipped backwards. He landed hard flat on his back on the ground. Air whooshed out of the guy. He lay there gasping for air. His hands fumbling away the ax handle.

Devon stood up. He grabbed the ax. As the soldier started struggling to get back up Devon whacked him across the face with the ax handle. The soldier wobbled and then sunk down to the ground. He lay there wheezing.

Moreland and Jessica stared at Devon. He looked back at them.

"I never really liked that guy." Devon said with a shrug.

Moreland stepped over to the soldier. She studied his face. "That's not the guy I saw where that girl was killed."

Devon glanced down at the soldier. "No. That's not Rico. This guy's name was Chad or something like that."

"What the hell? Is everyone trying to kill us?" Jessica asked.

Moreland shook her head. "I don't know, but I think we do need a gun."

"Along those lines, to answer your question a couple of minutes ago, I was trying to remember where we kept the ax we used to break up chunks of ice." Devon said.

"Did you remember?" Jessica asked.

Moreland turned to look at Jessica. "Really?"

"What?" Jessica asked.

Devon held up the ax. "Found it."

"Oh." Jessica said. "Yeah."

Devon led them back past Beecham's tent and into the fog in the direction he had pointed to earlier. After a few minutes walking a shape grew out of the mist. It was a small cinder block building. No windows. No signs. Only a steel door with a padlock.

"Oh. Didn't know this was out here." Moreland commented.

Devon shrugged. "Well, as a general rule, the Army doesn't usually tell everyone where the weapons are kept. Besides, like I said before, the expectation was that anything dangerous down here was long since dead."

Moreland and Jessica stepped back as Devon took a couple of swings at the padlock. The padlock dropped to the ground and Devon pulled the door open. Jessica peered in.

"It's dark in there." Jessica said. She looked at Devon. "Where's the light switch?"

Devon shook his head. He leaned past Jessica and felt around just inside the door. He found a switch and flipped it. Nothing happened. His hand searched around some more and came back with a flashlight.

"In the event the generators are down and there's no electricity." Devon said holding up the flashlight and then switching it on. Using the flashlight he found a second flashlight and handed it to Moreland.

They walked in. Devon flashed the light around. He seemed to find what he was looking for and pulled a small crate off a shelf. He pulled a handgun out of it, dug around and found the magazines for it. He loaded the weapon and held it up.

"This is an M18. It has a 17 round magazine containing 9mm cartridges. It's effective to about 25 yards." Devon said.

Jessica held out a hand. "Cool."

Moreland stepped in front of Jessica and took the gun. She looked at it briefly in the dim light from the door.

"Is that the safety?" Moreland pointed.

Devon nodded. "Yes."

Moreland made sure the safety was on and stuffed the gun into the waist of her jeans.

Devon did the same.

"What about me?" Jessica asked.

Moreland looked at Jessica. "The University of Chicago insurance plan specifically does not cover you carrying a gun."

Jessica studied Moreland for a moment. "I don't think the university insurance mentions me specifically." Jessica's voice lacked certainty.

Devon flashed the light quickly around the room. He seemed satisfied that this was all they needed.

"Hey, are there like grenades and shit like that in here?" Jessica asked. She scanned around the room.

"Let's go." Moreland said walking out of the weapons locker.

They started moving back in the general direction of the camp. It was hard in the fog to be completely sure you were going in a direct path to your destination. The markers helped, but there were no markers leading to the weapons locker.

They had only gone a short distance when Moreland reached out and pulled at Devon's sleeve.

"Wait, Scotty. Was the ice climbing stuff in the weapons locker?" Moreland asked.

Devon shook his head. "No ma'am. That stuff is in the supply tent."

Moreland just looked at Devon expectantly.

Devon hesitated. "Are you sure about that?"

Moreland shook her head slowly. "No, I'm not, but we can't stay here."

Again Devon hesitated and then pointed in a general direction. "The supply tent is on the other side of the dining tent."

Moreland held out a hand inviting Devon to lead.

Moreland started to follow Devon, but Jessica grabbed Moreland's arm.

"You're thinking we are going to climb out of this place?" Jessica asked.

"I don't think anyone's going to be coming any time soon to get us. We can't stay here. No one is operating that damned lift. So...I don't know of any other way out." Moreland said.

Moreland walked on so they didn't lose sight of Devon in the fog. She pulled Jessica along.

"Have you ever ice climbed before?" Jessica asked.

Moreland shook her head. "No. Have you?"

"Hell no. I don't even think I will know which end of the ice hooky thing to hold." Jessica said.

"Think of it as a big fork." Moreland said.

"Those hooky things are nothing like a—-wait, you're implying something, aren't you?" Jessica said.

They came up on the back side of a tent. It was the one next to Beecham's tent. Two down from the Admin tent. They walked between the tents and crossed the camp to the dining tent. Devon led them between another set of tents and a large tent emerged behind the others.

"Still no one here." Devon said. "There should be someone guarding the entrance at all times. Otherwise, well, things go missing."

Devon was about to step through the flaps of the supply tent, but he stopped. He pulled out his gun, checked it and then pushed through the flap.

There were pallets of boxes and various bins lining the walls of the tent. Some pallets were stacked nearly to the ceiling. There was some stuff dumped and scattered about. Someone had been in here. It was hard to tell if they were searching for something or just deliberating making a mess.

Devon crawled around some of the pallets towards the back of the tent. The ice climbing equipment was not in high demand so he knew they would buried somewhere. It took him a little while to locate the one box he was searching for. He couldn't uncover the box to pull it out, but he could cut the box open on one side and fish out what they needed. He turned and held up harnesses, ropes, ice axes and the crampons that would stretch over their boots and give them spikes for climbing ice.

Moreland and Jessica eyed the equipment.

"Have you ever done ice climbing?" Moreland asked. "A little late to ask, but..."

Devon shrugged. "Everyone got a basic training in it. So, I guess you could say I've done a little. Back home in Colorado I did some rock climbing. Not quite the same."

"Close enough. You've been promoted to climbing instructor." Moreland said.

They stepped out of the supply tent. Moreland glanced up at the fog above them.

"Not exactly sure what time it is." Moreland said.

"It's 4:37pm." Devon said looking at his watch.

Moreland turned to look at Devon. "How long do you think it will take us to make that climb?"

Devon thought for a minute. "Realistically? Hours."

"I don't think we have enough daylight left to start now." Moreland said.

"Well, this is a fine pickle." Jessica said.

Moreland and Devon looked at Jessica.

Jessica looked at them. "I don't want to do that ice climb. I don't even know if I can, but spending a dark night down here with people getting killed all over the place sounds even worse."

"Yeah." Moreland said. She glanced over in the direction of the camp. They could still here occasional crying, yelling and other assorted unsettling sounds.

"The weapons locker." Devon said.

"Yeah. Yeah, good idea Scotty. It's about the only truly solid structure I've seen here. And...you can show us how to use these things." Moreland nodded as she reached for harness and rotated it couple of times trying to see which way was up.

They walked back towards the camp. As they started past the dining tent Jessica slowed down.

"Hey, you know, maybe we should stock up a little. You know, on provisions." Jessica said looking at the dining tent.

Moreland was about to say something sarcastic, but realized she too was hungry. They hadn't eaten all day. Moreland knew she was something of a binge starver when she was stressed. A part of her suddenly recognized that it was somewhat amazing Jessica hadn't said something earlier.

"Probably a good idea." Moreland said.

Jessica just stood there looking at Moreland. She seemed to be waiting for some comment. She shrugged.

"Sweet." Jessica started towards the flap of the dining tent. Devon reached out and gently pulled her back a little. He pulled out his gun again, made eye contact with Jessica and stepped in front of her and through the flap.

There was no one in dining tent, which, under normal conditions, was very odd. There were two red emergency lights still on. They gave off enough light to navigate. The one generator was still running, but Devon suspected that a breaker for the dining tent had been tripped.

This place too looked like someone had decided to have a minor food fight. There were trays, silverware, glasses and mugs tossed all around. They wandered around the various upright coolers that held drinks, packaged sandwiches and a variety of dairy products. The lack of power from the generators had shut down the coolers, but the drop in temperature from the lack of running electric heaters kept everything naturally refrigerated.

Jessica was eating while she stuffed sandwiches into her pockets and just about every other place that would hold them. She jammed in a few cans of soda as well.

"You know the ropes are only rated for a few hundred pounds, right?" Moreland asked.

"What? Ropes? What about the ropes?" Jessica looked over at Moreland. She glanced down at the two sandwiches in her hands still waiting to find a home somewhere in her coat. "Hey, I'm going to need strength."

"Yeah, well there's such a thing as a point of diminishing returns, but whatever." Moreland said. None of the slowly aging sandwiches looked appealing to her, but she knew there was a grain of truth in what Jessica had said. She made herself pickup a sandwich. She studied it. It was a layer of something gray and with an additional thin layer of something beige. Neither one of those seemed like edible colors. She was sure she had studied sedimentary rock layers that looked more appetizing. With an effort she stuffed it into a pocket.

Devon too, selected a couple of sandwiches and tucked them away. He was accustomed to this fare and was less intimidated by it. The Army had a policy that if you were afraid of what the mess tent served they would find something for you to do that would scare you a lot more.

"We need to get going." Moreland said. She was growing increasingly nervous about making the climb now and couldn't really even think about eating. She was fast approaching the magic number of 40 and, never having been that athletic in the past, she harbored a fear that she was not going to be able make the climb.

"Just one more thing." Jessica hopped over to a stand where there snack cakes and snatched up one.

Moreland just watched her. "Don't forget a fork."

"A fork? Why...oh well, what the hell." Jessica yanked a metal fork out of the slot they were in. She stuffed it into her pocket and then glanced over at Moreland. "Wait, you were being sarcastic weren't you?"

Moreland just looked at Jessica.

Jessica shrugged and they headed out of the dining tent. They made their back to the weapons locker. Inside the locker only the two flashlights they had gave them any light. A quick inspection of the inside of the door revealed there was no means of locking the door from the inside.

"Seems like something of an oversight." Moreland said staring the door and then at Devon.

Devon shrugged. "Not really. Anyone that would lock themselves in a weapons locker is probably not the person you want locking themselves *in* a weapons locker."

Moreland nodded. "Right. I guess I get the logic there."

Devon found a rifle and jammed the butt of the rifle up under the handle of the door and into the dirt floor.

Devon glanced at Moreland shrugged. Moreland returned the shrug. It would have to do.

They pulled some boxes and a couple of tarps down off shelves to give them some kind of platform to lounge on while the night passed. After that they just sat for a few minutes in silence.

"We should probably turn these lights off. Save the batteries." Devon said.

"We have to sit in the dark?" Jessica asked.

"The batteries won't last all night." Moreland switching her flashlight off. Devon turned his off as well.

Quiet minutes passed. Then the sound of chewing could be heard.

"Really?" Moreland asked.

"I eat when I'm nervous. Darkness makes me nervous." Jessica said into the surrounding black.

It took a while for the three of them to drop off into an uneasy sleep. Claustrophobic hours passed.

"What the hell?" Moreland as all three of them jumped awake at the sound of a scream not far from the building.

"Shit." Jessica said.

There was some fumbling around and finally Moreland got her flashlight on. She shined it on the door. Devon was already leaning against the door with his gun ready. He was listening. He glanced back at Moreland and shook his head.

It took Moreland a moment to realize he was referring to the flashlight. She switched it off.

Minutes passed with no other sound. Slowly Devon made his way back to their makeshift sleeping platform. There was a general feeling that it would be very difficult to get back to sleep.

Moreland stared off into the darkness wondering how things could have devolved into such a nightmare in such a short period of time. She shook her head slowly and sat listening to Jessica chewing.

9

"OK. If we're going to do this we should get started." Moreland said as she glanced at the faintly glowing numbers on Devon's watch.

Moreland glanced in the direction of Jessica's quiet snoring. She nudged Jessica.

"What? Shoot it. Kill it." Jessica said as she jolted awake.

"Save your sound advice for when we need it." Moreland said as she got to her feet.

Devon stood up as well.

"What? It's only been a few minutes." Jessica said.

"A few hours, actually." Devon said.

"Huh." Jessica said. She stood up and reached into one of her pockets. "We should have some breakfast."

Moreland was going to comment on that and once again realized there was a certain logic to it. She, however, had little or no appetite.

"Have a little something. I'm going to take a look outside." Moreland said.

"I will join you ma'am." Devon said.

Outside Devon and Moreland glanced around in the dim light of the morning. Even in the midday light there wasn't much to see with the fog and they spent a few minutes just wandering around the weapons locker and listening. There seemed to be nothing stirring. It was almost as creepy as hearing someone screaming.

They went back into the weapons locker and gathered their climbing equipment as Jessica finished off another sandwich. The three of them left the small building and began walking back towards the camp. As they walked the metal parts of their climbing gear occasionally clinked and each time they looked around and at each other.

Something seemed to have changed during the night and now all three of them felt a need to be as quiet as possible. To keep a low profile.

They had made the decision to get out of the Trench and now that was their only priority.

When they reached the edge of the camp they stopped. Devon had been leading and he turned to look at Moreland. He gestured. He was wordlessly asking whether they should go around the outskirts of the camp or through it.

Moreland hesitated. The camp was utterly silent. That seemed odd considering there had been an almost constant background sound of people in some kind of distress for the last couple of days. After a minute of staring into the fog Moreland shrugged. She waved at Devon to go ahead. Straight through. It was the quickest way to where the lift was.

Devon turned and wove in between a couple of tents. They slowly walked down through the center of camp. There was trash and various debris from people's tents strewn about. A couple of times there looked to be a body laying just on the fringes of what they could clearly see in the fog. They didn't stop. Didn't investigate. They kept moving.

They exited the far side of the camp without encountering anything. Outside the camp Devon stopped. He stood for a moment glancing back at the vague shape of some tents in the camp and then out towards the fog.

"What is it?" Moreland asked. Her voice low.

Devon frowned. "I know this is the right direction, but it looks like someone has knocked the markers down. Or took them."

"You mean we could just get lost out there in the fog?" Jessica asked.

Devon shook his head. "No. I can find our way OK." He started off in a direction and Moreland and Jessica followed. Minutes passed. Moreland and Jessica gave each other quick glances as Devon made a couple of zigzag course corrections. Then suddenly, out of the fog, emerged framework of the lift.

"Wow, that was pretty good." Jessica said. Relief in her voice. "Thought we were lost."

Devon shrugged. "I used to do orienteering when I was a kid."

"You...went to, like, China?" Jessica asked.

Devon laughed a little. "No. You go out into the woods with just a compass and a crude map. It's like a race. You try to reach a designated point in the shortest time."

Jessica looked at him. "Why didn't you just—-oh, wait, Uber's don't go out into the woods, do they?"

Moreland sighed.

They circled the lift and walked a short distance further. The ice wall of the Trench loomed over them.

Jessica walked up to the wall and looked up. The fog prevented them from seeing very far up.

"How far up is it again?" Jessica asked.

Devon hesitated. He knew how high it was, but clearly didn't want to frighten Jessica.

"They said it was about a hundred feet." Moreland said.

"Shit." Jessica said.

Moreland looked at Devon. "No sense denying it. Might as well just rip the band aid off."

Devon helped them into their harnesses. As he tightened up Jessica's harness they looked at each other for just a moment.

"OK." Devon said standing with his back to the ice and looking at the two of them. "I will go up first and secure a couple of anchors and a second line. Whoever follows me snap yourself into the line I drop. When you get to the first anchor where the line is secured there will be another line. Transfer to that line. Do that for each anchor you come to. The third person will need to pull up the bottom two lines as they transfer to the next line. We don't have enough rope for the whole climb otherwise."

"What does the third person do, carry the ropes in their teeth?" Jessica asked.

"No." Devon said. "They just need to wrap the rope around themselves. Like this." He patted the ropes he had wrapped around his torso.

"Wrap the ropes…? I'm going to be hanging on for dear life up there." Jessica said.

Devon shook his head. "You don't need to put all your weight on your arms. You don't want to do that. Your arms will be like rubber after only about 20 feet. Your harness has the climber on it. You grip it, slide it up as you climb. When you release it, like I showed you, it will hold you. You can't slide back down the rope. Just lean back in the harness and wrap the rope."

Jessica looked worried.

"I'll take the third position." Moreland said. "I'll pull the ropes."

Jessica looked slightly relieved.

"OK. At one of our rest stops, about half way up, I will need you to transfer those ropes to me." Devon said.

Moreland nodded.

"Ready?" Devon asked.

"As ready as I can be." Moreland said.

Jessica just stared at the ice wall and slowly shook her head.

Devon started up the wall while Jessica and Moreland watched him until he dissolved into the fog.

"I feel like I'm going to throw up." Jessica said.

"Don't you dare." Moreland said.

"It would lighten the load as I went." Jessica said.

"I will be below you. If you vomit on me you better climb like hell because I am coming after you with one of these ax things." Moreland waving an ice ax at her.

"Oh Jesus!" Jessica jumped as a rope suddenly snapped next to her. It danced around for a moment.

"OK. Jessica start now." Devon's voice came out of the fog above.

Jessica stared at the rope. "Didn't need that. I'm nervous enough as it is. Let me shake the shit out of my pants first."

"Oh, I didn't need to hear that." Moreland said. She stepped forward and snapped Jessica on to the rope. "You can do it."

It took a couple of minutes and help from Moreland for Jessica to slowly get a feel for the sequence for each ice cleated foot and ax wielding hand. At a snail's pace she crept up the wall.

Just before the fog engulfed Jessica she turned back to look at Moreland. There was an obvious fearful hesitation at sliding into the fog. Once there each one of them would largely be isolated and alone.

Moreland nodded up at Jessica. "Don't stop for sandwiches."

"Fuck you." Jessica gave Moreland a quick smile. Minutes later Jessica had disappeared.

Moreland waited. Occasionally she turned to look back in the direction of the camp. It was creepy now to stand all alone there after all that had happened. She struggled to keep the idea that some crazed killer was about to burst out of the fog at her.

After a little while she could hear voices. She recognized Devon's voice asking Jessica how she was doing and something about transferring from one rope to another.

Several minutes later Moreland could here Jessica's voice.

"You're up, Doc." Jessica shouted down to Moreland.

Moreland took a deep breath and started up the rope. She knew this was going to be physically taxing and was unpleasantly surprised to find that it was even more difficult than she was expecting. She moved slowly and it seemed to her that she was going even slower than Jessica had. She was glad Jessica couldn't see her because, if she could, Moreland knew she would never hear the end of it.

It took all of her concentration to keep herself coordinated. If you got out of sequence on moving a hand or foot you were forced into a very awkward slow dance to get your weight shifted back into a manageable position. After what seemed like forever she came up on the first anchor.

Moreland buried her ice ax into the wall and started to unhook herself to transfer to the next rope above. She caught herself before she clicked on the upper rope. She looked up.

"Jessica, are you on the next rope?" Moreland called up.

It took a moment for Jessica to answer.

"What? Hell yes. Are you just getting to the anchory thing?" Jessica yelled down.

"Uh, just checking." Moreland said. Moreland decided to avoid answering Jessica's question. She clicked on to the next rope and worked herself up a couple of feet. It took her a little while to untie the knot and pull up the lower rope. She wound it around herself. She started up and immediately and sadly realized that rope weighed more than she thought it should.

Moreland crawled slowly up the second rope. She could hear voices above her as progressed up. Nearing the top end of the second rope both Jessica and Devon came into view. Devon had them connected to their own separate anchors.

Moreland pulled up to the anchor of the second rope.

Jessica looked over at Moreland. "Man, you're moving slow."

"I doing just fine." Moreland said a little indignantly.

"No, I mean it. I've seen smashed turtles move faster than that." Jessica said.

"Don't you have a sandwich to eat?" Moreland said.

Jessica's face lit up. "Oh, yeah. I forgot about them." Jessica said reaching into a pocket.

"What's gotten into you anyway? You were all worked up about doing this climb and now you're fired up." Moreland said.

Jessica smiled at Moreland. "I am the fucking ice climbing queen."

Moreland stared at her for a moment and then looked at Devon.

Devon shrugged. "She's a natural. Who knew?"

They rested for a little while longer until Moreland assured Devon she was ready.

"So, we're going to stop at the next anchor up again. That way you only have to carry the one rope." Devon said looking at Moreland. "When we get there you pass me the rope you're carrying. Then transfer from the rope to the rope anchor. Then pull up the rope you were just on and hand that one to me too. Then you and Jessica wait on the anchors until I get the next rope set. Got it?"

Moreland nodded. "Got it." She was relieved she wouldn't have to carry two ropes. She knew the weight of the second rope would slow her down even more. She didn't know what might be slower than a smashed turtle, but she didn't want to be it—-whatever it was.

At the next anchor point Moreland worked through the rope transfers. Devon took both ropes and worked his way up to set the next rope. He was lost in the fog within a few minutes. Jessica and Moreland hung on their respective anchors and waited.

"You're doing great." Moreland said. She tried to hide how winded she was as she spoke.

Jessica smiled. "Oh hell yes. I'm killing it." Jessica glanced down. "It helps a lot that I can't see how high we are."

Moreland nodded. "Yeah."

They waited and started to feel the cold creep in. While climbing they were exerting themselves to the point of sweating, but once they stopped even briefly they could feel the cold work its way into them. They hung within inches of an inconceivable amount of ice that could easily suck every bit of heat out of them in a short period of time.

It seemed to Moreland that Devon was taking longer to set the rope than usual and she couldn't help running through a list in her head of the various really bad things that could still happen to them as hung on the side of a cliff of ice.

"Ow!" Jessica said as the rope dropped down slapped her on the head. "Damn it, Scotty."

Jessica snapped on to the rope and started up. Moreland continued to hang on her anchor trying to shake an image in her head of being hung in a meat locker on a hook.

Again, it seemed like Jessica was taking longer to scale the rope than previous segments. Finally, Moreland heard Jessica call down to come up. She clicked her climber on the rope and started up.

About half way up Moreland came upon the end of a second rope. It was hanging next to the rope she was on. That seemed odd. She couldn't think of a reason that Devon would have overlapped the ropes. After a few minutes it occurred to Moreland what was going on. They were nearly at the top and only needed a short length to get up there. She smiled and the thought gave her an energy burst. She worked a little faster, despite being very tired, to get to the top of the current rope.

As she drew nearer the other two, Moreland could hear a quietly intense conversation. She couldn't quite make out the details, but it sounded like Jessica was unhappy about something.

When Moreland was close enough to see Devon and Jessica neither one of them seemed very happy. That seemed strange to Moreland considering how close they were to the top. As Moreland pulled herself to the top of her rope she saw the difference between their expressions. Devon seemed to be worried. Jessica was clearly afraid.

"What? What's wrong?" Moreland asked.

"We can't get up there." Jessica said.

"What?" Moreland asked. "What do you mean?"

Devon sighed. "There's an overhang."

"Overhang." Moreland said the word and started processing what it meant. "You mean the ice sticks out?" She waved her hand out away from the wall.

Devon nodded.

"How far?" Moreland asked, but her gut told her even a couple of feet would make the climb immensely more difficult.

"About six feet." Devon said.

"Shit." Moreland said. "Can we get around it?"

Devon shook his head. "I don't think so. At least, not without taking a while to scout out a route. And..."

"And what?" Moreland asked.

"We would need to guess at which direction to try." Devon said.

Moreland glanced left and right. Shit, she thought, he's right. Can't see damned thing in this fog. It would be a 50-50 gamble they picked a direction that might get them around the overhang.

"Is...there a way to get past it?" Moreland asked. She was afraid of the answer.

"I...don't know. I didn't get training on that kind of thing." Devon said. There was a clear trace of fear in Devon's voice.

"Shit. Shit." Moreland said. If they couldn't go up here they would have to go all the way back down and tomorrow move to another section of wall and blindly climb again in the hope they didn't run into this again.

They sat silently for a couple of minutes. Jessica sniffled a little. She was clearly on the verge of sobbing.

Moreland looked at Devon. It was a hard look. "The person that first went up there would have to climb upside down, right?"

Devon nodded. "I believe so."

"With no rope. Free climb it." Moreland said.

Devon nodded again.

"What if you put in two anchors below the overhang and tied yourself to both anchors and then tried climbing out and over the edge? So, if you fell the anchors would stop you." Moreland asked.

Devon's was nervous, but he nodded as he thought about it. "I guess..."

Feared swirled in her guts as Moreland thought about what she was suggesting he try to do.

"You...would have to...hang from the ice axes...like, one at a time..." Moreland said, articulating what no one wanted to hear.

"Oh, God, Scotty, no." Jessica said.

"If we go back down, I don't know if I would have the strength to climb back up here." Moreland said.

"Then we just go back down and wait for help." Jessica said.

Moreland shook her head. "If we stay down there, sooner or later, whoever or whatever is killing people there is bound to catch up with us too."

"I'll go." Devon said.

"Scotty, no." Jessica pleaded.

Devon shook his head. "No. It has to be done and I'm the only one that realistically has a chance of doing it."

"What if we help hold you up while you climbed?" Jessica asked.

Devon shook his head again. "No. You two will have to stay here."

"Stay here? No." Jessica said.

"Yes." Devon said firmly. "If I do fall and collide with one of you, well, that wouldn't be good."

They were all silent for a moment.

"OK. I need to get going. We can't hang here long. We'll freeze." Devon said.

"Scotty." Jessica said. She reached over and pulled him closer to her. They hugged as much as their respective anchors would allow.

When they let go Moreland reached across Jessica and grabbed Devon's arm. "Needless to say, be careful. Also...if you do fall and you're hurt..."

Devon nodded. "I know."

"Know what?" Jessica asked.

Devon put a hand on Jessica's shoulder and then turned and started climbing. When Devon had disappeared into the fog Jessica turned to Moreland.

"What was that about?" Jessica asked.

Moreland hesitated, but she knew Jessica needed to hear it.

"If he falls he will crash into the ice wall. If he is seriously injured. I...don't know if we could get him back down." Moreland said.

"What? No, if Scotty is hurt we will get his ass back down from this fucking ice shit." Jessica said.

Moreland knew that realistically it might be physically more than the two of them could do, but she also knew that, in her heart, she couldn't leave him up here to die either.

"OK." Moreland said.

They hung there in silence. Ever sound they could hear only made the tension worse. They could hear the tapping Devon was doing planting the two anchors into the ice. Then nothing for a little while.

"Damn it, what's happening?" Jessica said in frustration.

"I'm sure he's taking his time and working carefully." Moreland said trying to sound comforting. It didn't sound all that comforting and she knew she wasn't really very good at that kind of thing.

Jessica sighed and stared up into the fog.

Suddenly there was a clanking sound and some other muffled noise that almost sounded like words.

It took Moreland a minute to realize the clanking sound was ice axes bouncing off the wall. Her stomach clenched. It meant that Devon likely fell. She wanted to call up to him, but was afraid that she wouldn't get a response.

It took Jessica a minute longer to figure out the sound. "Scotty? Scotty?" She called out.

"I'm OK." Came Devon's voice from above. "I'm starting again."

Jessica was about to say something, but Moreland reached out and grabbed her arm.

"He's OK. Let him concentrate." Moreland said.

Jessica hesitated and then nodded. They hung in silence for a while again. It was nerve wracking. Finally Jessica couldn't take it anymore.

"Why haven't we heard anything?" Jessica asked anxiously.

"That's a good sign." Moreland said. "It means he's making progress."

Moreland really didn't know that was true, but there was a certain logic to it.

"I guess." Jessica said.

They waited again. Then a snapping sound cracked next to Moreland. A rope. Jessica and Moreland exchanged glances.

"Holy shit. Did he do it?" Jessica asked excitedly.

Devon's voice called down to start up.

Moreland and Jessica smiled at each other.

"Oh, thank God." Moreland said. "Let me see if I can get this rope over to you."

"That's OK. Just go." Jessica said.

"Are you sure?" Moreland asked.

Jessica nodded. "I'm fine. Now that I know he's OK. Well, and that we are getting the hell out of here. You go. I'll follow."

Moreland nodded. She snapped on to the rope and began the ascent. She was nearly completely lost in the fog when she could hear Jessica laugh.

"Go, smashed turtle, go."

"Fuck you." Moreland said quietly, laughing a little.

The higher Moreland got the more something seemed messed up. The rope was getting in here way. She kept having to shove it out of her face. She stopped and stared at the situation. It suddenly struck her that the rope was not hugging the wall as usual.

Of course, idiot, she thought, the rope is out on the edge of the overhang. With that thought, though, came a scary understanding of what would have to come next. She was going to have to let go of the wall and just hang freely on the rope. Her ice axes and the spikes on her boots were now going to be useless to her.

Moreland took a deep breath. No way around this. She let the ice axes dangle down and eased her feet away from the wall. She slowly spun in the air. Oh God, I might be the one doing the shitting, she thought.

She now had to work the rope climber up above her and slowly begin pulling herself up the rope. It didn't take long for her arms really feel the burn. Without her feet to help support her weight it was all on her arms. Come on, you little paleontological stick arms, work, she told herself.

Moreland was so focused on the climb that Devon's voice surprised her.

"Go Doc." Devon said smiling down at her from the edge.

She glanced up at him with a smile and then at the ice wall. It looked like it was fifty feet away. She knew it was only about six feet, but hanging on a rope everything seemed far away.

Devon reached down and started helping her up over the edge of the overhang. When she crawled up on top of the overhang there was a massive sense of relief, but also a creepy feeling. The top of the overhang was not flat. It was sloped. Sloping ice was very hard to navigate.

Devon helped Moreland up a short way and then clicked her into an anchor he had in place for her.

Moreland lowered her head to the ice and just breathed. She heard Devon call down to Jessica to start up.

After a couple of minutes Moreland lifted her head up. It was then she realized that it seemed brighter here. She looked up. Through a haze of fog she could see blue sky. Her eyes teared a little. It was amazing how much being able to just see the sky meant to her. She didn't know how much she missed it. She took a deep breath and smiled.

"You're swinging the rope a lot." Devon said.

Moreland glanced down the sloping ice. Devon was laying on his stomach again peering over the edge. He was talking to Jessica. A moment later Moreland could see Jessica's head appear over the edge of the overhang.

Devon reached over and grabbed one of Jessica's arms to help her clear the edge. Jessica grinned at Moreland.

In an instant things happened fast. Jessica had gotten her upper half over the edge. She had crawled past the point at which Devon, still laying on his stomach, could grip her left arm. There was a snap as the rope Jessica was on, frayed by the edge of the overhang, separated. Jessica felt the support of the rope disappear and her face flashed a look of horror.

Moreland spun around and tried to grab at Jessica's outstretched left hand, but couldn't get a hold before Jessica started sliding back down the slope. Jessica snagged the remaining rope that was still connected to the anchor, but her weight was more than her grip on the snow covered rope could hold. The rope rapidly just slid through her glove.

Devon knew what was happening and had grabbed the only thing next to him which was a section of Jessica's coat, but he could feel that he was not going to be able to hold her once she slid over the edge.

Jessica's head and arms were the only things now still visible above the edge. Her left hand was flat against the ice achieving nothing as it slid along. Devon had already lost his grip on her.

"Jess..." Devon cried.

Moreland watched a blur of motion as Jessica's right arm as it arced around to the icy slope. There was a loud clink and for a just a moment Jessica stopped sliding. In that instant Devon lunged and got both hands on Jessica's left arm. He gripped with everything he still had in him.

Moreland stared. If her blood wasn't still filled with fear driven adrenaline she would have laughed. Stuck in the ice, with Jessica's right hand tightly gripping it, was a fork from the dining tent.

Jessica's eyes met Moreland's. "Fucking ice climbing queen." Jessica said.

Moreland disconnected from the anchor she was on and slid down the ice. She snapped her climber on to the remaining rope Jessica had been on. She could reached down from there and grab Jessica's right arm. With both Devon and Moreland pulling, Jessica cleared the edge of the overhang. She pulled herself up the rope Moreland was on and snapped into the anchor Moreland had disconnected from. Devon crawled back up to his own anchor.

All three of them exchanged a look of incredible relief and lay back on the ice resting.

"I'll be damned. Blue sky." Jessica said staring upward.

"Yeah." Moreland said. "What a beautiful thing."

10

"I'd almost forgotten what the sky looked like." Devon said laying on his back on the ice.

"Yeah, but my ass is starting to freeze." Jessica said.

"Right." Moreland said rotating around on to her knees. "We need to get...what the hell?"

Devon and Jessica both sat up and looked over at Moreland. She was staring up at the ice wall still above them.

"Oh, shit." Jessica said as she and Devon turned and looked up at the soldier standing at the top pointing a gun at them.

"I'm Private Devon." Devon called up to the soldier. "I'm escorting two civilians back up to camp."

The soldier didn't say anything. He seemed to be swaying slightly. He leaned forward as if he was trying to get a better look at them. The gun came forward too and he was clearly trying take aim on them.

A shot rang out and both Jessica and Moreland jumped at the sound. The soldier staggered forward and then slowly leaned over the edge until he dropped head first towards them. His body slammed into the icy slope a short distance in front of Jessica. For a moment no one moved. Then, the only person that shouldn't be moving did so. The soldier's body eased forward sliding down the slope picking up speed as it went. It slid between Moreland and Jessica and then disappeared over the edge of the overhang.

The three of them watched the body go. Jessica and Moreland looked over at Devon. He had slid his gun out as soon as he had seen the soldier. At this point none of them felt they could trust anyone they encountered.

Jessica looked up at the wide streak of blood the dead soldier left in front of them. She pointed. "I ain't climbing through that."

The soldier triggered an urgency on their part to get up to the top mixed with a certain level of fear at what they might find there.

Devon got moving. He began working his way up to the top. Once there he took a minute to scan the area. Satisfied that no one else was nearby he anchored a rope dropped it down. Minutes later Jessica was up and at smashed turtle speed Moreland, too, reached the top.

The three of them stood in the sunshine and stared out at the upper camp. It was a strange and eerie sight. Nothing seemed to be stirring. The last time they were here there was a constant flow of activity. Now, nothing.

In addition, it looked as though some kind of battle had taken place. From where they stood they could see bodies laying around the camp. Quite a few tents had been torn down or slashed open. A couple of fires burned with no one attempting to put them out.

"I don't think we're going to get any help here." Jessica said surveying the scene.

Moreland sighed. "It doesn't look very promising."

Slowly they walked side by side into the camp carefully scanning in all directions. Both Moreland and Devon had their guns out with Jessica between them.

They had only gone a short distance in when, from behind them, they heard a scraping sound. Turning they saw a soldier had emerged from the dining tent. His uniform was stained with blood. It could not have been solely his blood. No one having lost that much blood could still be moving. In his right hand he carried a meat cleaver. He limped as he walked. It was the dragging of his right foot that made the scraping sound.

Devon lifted his gun. "Stop! Stop or I'll shoot."

The soldier seemed not to notice. He kept moving towards them. His eyes seemed glazed over and fixed on them.

The soldier got within a dozen feet and Devon fired twice. The first shot caught the soldier in the shoulder, but appeared to have no effect. Devon's second shot went through the soldier's face and he dropped.

They watched the soldier's body for a moment, but there was no movement.

"Well, that's just fucking great." Jessica said. "They have their own crazed killer up here too."

Moreland looked around. She thought about what they had seen below. "This...doesn't seem like just one person."

"What do you mean?" Devon asked.

Moreland shrugged. "I don't know. Do you know where Major Wilkins' tent is?"

Devon slowly turned trying to remember from the last time he had been up here. "There, I think." He pointed back behind them.

"Let's go there first." Moreland said and the three of them headed back in that direction.

When Devon was sure of which tent it was they cautiously entered the tent. It was a mess. In the corner, half under a cot, was a body lying face down. Devon eased over to it and slowly turned it over. It wasn't Wilkins.

Moreland hoped there was still a chance they would find Wilkins somewhere. Obviously, though, not in here. She stepped over to the folding table that served as Wilkins' desk. It had drawn her attention because of what lay right in the center of it. Something told her that Wilkins left it and it was meant for them, well, someone, to find.

There was a knife stuck into an open book. Moreland looked more closely. The Bible. Old Testament. It was Ezekiel, chapters 8 and 9. It was about the destruction of Jerusalem. Without thinking Moreland placed a finger on a line and read it.

"Then he said to them, 'Defile the house, and fill the courts with the slain. Go forth.' So they went forth and smote the city." Moreland read.

"OK. That's some pretty creepy shit." Jessica said, suddenly standing next to Moreland.

Moreland nodded solemnly. "Yeah." She glanced over at Devon. "Didn't really take the Major as the religious type."

Devon shrugged.

They walked out of the tent.

"Now what?" Jessica asked.

"The radio." Moreland said. She looked at Devon.

Devon thought for a moment. He pointed to the left. "I think it's over there."

They moved in that direction. They had gone several more steps when there was a grunt to their left. From between a couple of tents another soldier staggered out. He was not looking at the three of them. He seemed to be staring straight ahead with no clear intent. After a couple of steps more he seemed to notice them. He turned and stared at them.

"Oh, God." Jessica said.

The left side of the soldier's face was badly mangled. It looked like he had been shot in the face. He started walking in their direction.

This time Moreland started firing first. Her shots were going everywhere except into the soldier.

"What the hell are you aiming at?" Jessica asked loudly.

Devon fired several shots, two of which struck the soldier.

The soldier stopped. Stood for a moment looking at them curiously and dropped dead.

Jessica looked at Moreland. "You shoot a gun like a smashed turtle too."

Moreland held up the gun and was about to say something and then changed her mind. "That doesn't make any sense at all."

"I just mean—-" Jessica started.

"I know what you meant." Moreland said indignantly. "It's not like I regularly have to shoot things. I'm a paleontologist. Everything's already dead when I get to it."

Jessica held out her hand. It was obvious she was waiting for the gun.

"Oh, no." Moreland said.

"Hey," Jessica said, "I'm the fucking ice climbing queen."

Moreland thought about it for a moment. Slowly she handed the gun over to Jessica. "But if you accidentally shoot me, I'm failing you this semester."

Jessica took the gun. "Deal."

They turned and continued on. It took them three tries to find the communications tent. When they walked in it was immediately apparent it was a waste of time. The equipment had been smashed. Debris was spread all around the tent.

They stepped back out into the camp and stood staring at the scene.

"So, we're back to now what?" Jessica said. "Can't we just walk back to the main camp?"

Devon shook his head. "Too far. But there might be a vehicle here somewhere that could get us there."

"Well, OK, then. Let's go find our ride." Jessica said. She turned and noticed Moreland had wandered off a short ways. She seemed to be looking the dead bodies that were strewn about.

"Hey, Doc, don't go far. We don't know how many crazed killers there are around here." Jessica said.

Moreland turned to look back at Jessica and Devon. She didn't say anything, but it was obvious something was on her mind.

Jessica and Devon walked over to her.

"What?" Jessica asked.

"These people..." Moreland waved a hand around. "A lot of them are armed."

Devon looked around. "Hmm, yeah. They must have been fighting something."

Moreland shook her head. "I...don't think so." Moreland took a few more steps away and looked at a couple more bodies. They were almost intertwined. Both dead.

"I...think these people killed each other." Moreland said.

"What?" Jessica said. "Like some crazy killing frenzy? Why would they do that?"

"I don't know." Moreland said. She scanned out across the camp.

"What they just all decided to ripping and tearing at each other?" Jessica shook her head. "That doesn't make any sense."

Moreland froze. She looked at Jessica and then turned to stare at the crane sitting on the edge of the Trench.

"Oh, my God." Moreland said.

"What?" Jessica asked.

"The Morrosaurus." Moreland said.

"Huh?" Jessica said. "They didn't kill anyone. They're all dead."

"It was them." Moreland said.

"What are you talking about?" Jessica asked.

"The Morrosaurus. They weren't killed by some predator. They killed each other." Moreland looked at Jessica. "Don't you remember? The marks on their bones. They weren't the teeth marks of a predator. They were the claws of other Morrosaurus."

"I said that and you told me I was crazy." Jessica said. "Huh, I'm a paleontological genius too."

Moreland frowned at her. "That would be a bit of a stretch. Anyway, something drove them to kill each other."

"Oh, shit." Devon said.

Jessica turned to look at him. "What's wrong?"

Devon looked past Jessica at Moreland. "You...think what made those dinosaurs kill each other..." he didn't finish his sentence. He just turned and took in the scene all around them.

"Yeah." Moreland said. "Whatever made the Morrosaurus kill each other made these people do it too."

"What...could do such a thing?" Jessica asked. She too was now staring at the state of the camp.

"I don't know. Something viral, I guess." Moreland said.

"A virus from millions of years ago? They can't live that long, can they?" Jessica asked.

Moreland thought for minute. "It's not unheard of."

The three of them stood silently for a couple of minutes.

"Shit." Jessica said.

Moreland looked at Jessica. "What?"

"If...there is some kind of virus and...it makes people go crazy and...start killing people..." Jessica said.

"Then we have been exposed to it too." Devon said.

"Yeah. We have to assume that it's in us too." Moreland said.

"Are we going to go crazy and kill each other?" Jessica's voice was rising.

Moreland sighed. "I don't know. I don't know what the incubation period would be for this thing. But..."

"What?" Jessica asked. Her voice held a some panic.

"If this thing ripped through two full camps killing everyone and we are carrying the virus..." Moreland said.

"We can't go to the Main camp." Devon finished her thought.

"What does that mean? We just...wait here until we turn into what? Crazed killer zombies?" Jessica was visibly shaking now.

Moreland didn't answer immediately. When she did speak, her voice quivered a little. "We can't let this virus spread beyond here."

All three of them exchanged a look. Slowly Moreland's eyes rested on Devon's gun.

"Oh shit, no. No, please God, no." Jessica cried.

The wind picked up as a low pressure system moved into the area. Heavy clouds rolled in from the south. From even a short distance away from the camp the sound of gun shots were lost.

Part 2 – Deja Vu

1

He never felt the bullet go through his brain. He saw the two women laying down on the ground. Who they were was now beyond his ability to determine. As darkness now swept through his brain he swayed a little and then, eternal darkness. His body dropped to the ground. The gun in his hand falling away. The camp was suddenly very quiet.

"What the fuck?" Jessica said. She sat up.

"Sorry, he just seemed to appear out of nowhere." Devon said.

"Maybe next time give us a little heads up before you just shove us to the ground." Moreland said brushing snow off her face.

"Yes ma'am." Devon said.

"Whoa, Scotty, you got him right in the head." Jessica said. "Oh, and it's pretty gross."

Devon shrugged. "It was kind of a lucky shot."

"Anyway, where were we?" Moreland asked.

"Oh, yeah. You were suggesting we off ourselves which I think is just stupid." Jessica said. "When they close the casket on me I'm going to still be kicking and screaming."

"Why would they put you in a casket if you were still alive?" Moreland asked looking at Jessica.

Jessica thought for a moment. "Hmm, yeah, that doesn't really sound right does it? Well, you know what I mean."

Moreland shook her head. "No, not really, but never mind."

"Ma'am?" Devon asked.

"Yeah, Scotty?" Moreland replied.

"How do we know the virus isn't already back at the Main camp or even back in McMurdo?" Devon asked.

Moreland stared at Devon. "Yeah...guess we don't. OK. I might have been jumping the gun on that one, but somehow, whatever this is, well, it just can't let it get out into the general population."

From somewhere to Moreland's right there was a loud smacking sound. Jessica whipped her gun out and wildly started firing in that direction. Moreland ducked down to one knee.

All three of them looked over to where a tent had collapsed on its own. Moreland turned to look at Jessica.

"What the hell, girl?" Moreland said.

"I thought it was one of those killer zombie things." Jessica said. "And you can't fail me because I didn't shoot you."

Moreland stood up. "Maybe not, but I sure as hell can assign you a shit ton of extra credit work."

"I think the vehicles are parked over there." Devon pointed.

They walked carefully on through the camp. Beyond some tents on the north side they saw a couple of military vehicles. They had a short front and two large forward facing windows. The back, a heavy canvas stretched over a frame, seemed to be suited for carrying supplies, equipment or a handful of soldiers. The closest one appeared to be in bad shape. As they got closer it was apparent that the nearest vehicle had been burned. There was no way that thing was ever going to run again.

They moved to the other vehicle. Devon looked the inside.

"Looks OK." Devon said looking inside.

"It's a funny looking truck." Jessica said.

"It's an LMTV." Devon said as he pulled himself into the driver's seat.

Jessica just stared at him.

"It's a Light Medium Tactical Vehicle." Devon said looking down at her.

Jessica shrugged. "I'm going to stick with funny looking truck."

"Can you drive it?" Moreland asked.

Devon glanced around at the console and nodded. "Yeah. These come in a few varieties. I haven't driven this particular one, but they are all about the same."

Jessica pulled herself up on the step and looked inside. "Hey, there's radio in here. Can't we just call the Main camp? Tell them to come get us?"

Devon shook his head. "This radio doesn't have the range to reach the Main camp. Part of the problem, I guess, has to do with being closer to the South Pole. I heard a couple of the communication guys talking. Something about an increase in the magnetism down here. To get a clear enough signal you need those small satellite dishes." Devon pointed up at the roof of the LMTV. "No dish on top of this."

"So I guess we are just driving all the way back." Moreland said standing next to the LMTV and watching for any trouble.

"We will need to stock up on fuel and a little luck." Devon said.

"I don't really want to ask this, but why do we need luck?" Moreland asked.

"Well, there's cleared path along the ice back to the Main camp, but it needs regular maintenance. So...it kind of depends on whether anyone has been out there recently to make sure it's clear." Devon said.

"Clear? Of what? It's a big sheet of ice." Jessica said.

Devon shook his head. "Not exactly. I mean, it is, but the ice sheet tends to buckle in places and create ridges. Some of the ridges we can get over. Others, well, not so much. They usually have to blast those out of the way."

"Of course." Moreland. "Always something. Why can't we just jump on the highway and zip on back to the Main camp."

"There's a highway out here?" Jessica asked. She turned and looked at Moreland.

Moreland just stared back at her.

Jessica sighed. "Fucking sarcasm."

"First issue will be," Devon pulled the visor down on the front window and a set of keys hit him in the head, "keys."

"Nice find." Jessica said.

Devon looked at Jessica. "Thanks." He put the keys in and turned on the electrical power to the LMTV. He stared at the gauges for just a moment. "Low on fuel."

"Where's the gas station?" Jessica asked.

"The fuel depot is somewhere past those two buildings." Devon pointed.

"OK, then. Let's go get gassed up." Jessica said.

"We have to let the diesel fuel warm up." Devon said. He glanced around and then flipped a switch. "OK. That will need a little time to heat up.

"Let's go check on the fuel depot." Devon said and both he and Jessica climbed down from the LMTV.

Moreland and Jessica followed Devon around a couple of quonset huts. As they turned a corner and came into sight of the fuel depot it was apparent they had a bigger problem. In retrospect, they realized they could smell the problem before they saw it.

The building where the fuel was kept was nothing more than a charred ruin. There was area of black ice surrounding the building where diesel fuel had run out across the ice and burned. They stood staring at it.

"Shit." Moreland said. She turned to Devon. "Is there any other place we could get fuel here?"

Devon shook his head. He didn't say anything.

"Does that truck thing have enough fuel to get us to the Main camp?" Moreland knew the answer to the question, but asked it anyway just in case there was a different answer she might miraculously get.

Again Devon shook his head.

"Shit." Moreland said. "So we can't call them and we can't drive there."

Devon nodded. "That's about it."

"Can't we just shoot up flares or something? You know, so they know someone is here and needs help?" Jessica asked.

"We're too far away for them to see it from the Main camp." Devon said.

"What if we got closer?" Moreland asked. "Could that truck thing—-"

"LMTV." Devon said absently.

"Yeah, LM whatever. That thing. Could that get us close enough for them to see flares?"

Devon sighed. "I doubt it. Unless...maybe if they have any helicopters up. Then maybe."

"Well, it's better than sitting here waiting for killer zombies to get us." Jessica said.

"I agree." Moreland said.

"OK." Devon said. He didn't sound like he had a lot of faith that plan would work.

"OK. So where do we find flares?" Moreland asked.

Devon waved a hand back towards the center of the camp. "Supply tent. It's back there."

Moreland stepped over to Devon. She put a hand on his shoulder. "We just have to keep going. We don't have any other choice."

Devon nodded. "Yes ma'am." He took a deep breath and seemed to clear his head.

They headed back into the camp and Devon looked around. He spotted what he was looking for. It was the top of a larger building. They navigated to it. They circled around the building to the door that now hung open. Devon pulled his gun back out and stepped into the building first. Jessica and Moreland followed. It was quiet and seemingly empty.

There were considerably more supplies here than the supply tent down in the Trench. Like below there were pallets, bins and, in here, some actual pieces of equipment. They spread out and began searching. Jessica gravitated towards a section that clearly held food supplies for the camp.

It took a little while of rummaging through the pallets and boxes before Devon found the flares. He held them up.

"Nice." Moreland said. "I found some blankets here and I was thinking we might want to take some with us."

Devon nodded. "That's probably a good idea."

Moreland pulled a few blankets out. She wondered what Jessica was getting and then realized what Jessica was probably doing. She wandered around a couple of stacks of pallets. She turned a corner and, sure enough, there was Jessica sitting on the floor holding a couple of prepackaged sandwiches in her hands.

Moreland was about to say something when the scene seemed odd. Jessica was just sitting there. A sandwich in each hand as they rested on her lap. She wasn't eating.

"What's the deal? Those sandwiches won't eat themselves." Moreland said.

Jessica looked up at Moreland and then down at the sandwiches. "Oh, I don't know. I guess I'm a little tired."

Moreland knelt down next to Jessica. She studied Jessica more closely. She put a hand on Jessica's forehead.

"Son of a bitch." Moreland said.

"What?" Jessica said.

"You have fever." Moreland said.

Devon appeared from around another corner. "What?"

Moreland looked at Devon. There was fear in her eyes. "She's got a fever."

Moreland could see alarm in Devon's eyes.

Jessica looked at both of them. "What? You think I'm sick? I'm fine. I...I just need a little rest. That's all."

"We need to haul ass to the Main camp." Moreland said.

"Why? I mean, I'm...well, OK, maybe, I mean, they probably already have a cure for this thing, right?" Jessica said.

"I'm sure they do by now." Moreland said.

Jessica looked at Moreland. "You suck at lying. I think I like your sarcasm better."

Moreland stood up. She looked at Devon. "We need to get going."

Devon nodded. "I agree." Devon's voice was hesitant.

"What?" Moreland asked. "Don't tell we have another problem because I am just about fed up with new problems."

Devon shook his head a little. "No. It's just that it's getting late. We won't get too far before darkness comes and we can't travel at night. Too dangerous."

"I don't want to stay in this place for the night." Jessica said slowly getting to her feet.

"OK." Moreland said. "Let's drive out away from this camp and then push on as soon as it is light enough."

They carried their supplies back to the LMTV. Devon got the engine started and slowly eased the vehicle through the camp. A couple of times the LMTV bumped over something. The second time they went over a bump something registered in Jessica's head.

"Wait, did you just run over a body?" Jessica asked.

Devon glanced over at her. "Maybe."

"Oh, that's creepy. Don't do that. It's gross." Jessica said.

"I'm trying not to, but...they're like, everywhere." Devon said.

As soon as they cleared the camp Devon picked up a little speed. Not much because he had to watch for uneven ice or, even worse, open crevices. It was difficult to stare out at the ice for anything length of time. It was white on white. After a short while all of the white in front of them looked like one big blur.

Darkness crept up on them and Devon finally stopped. They hunkered down under blankets and Jessica magically made sandwiches appear from various pockets in her coat. After that they did their best to try to get some rest. They could feel the cold slowly creeping into the LMTV. It was not going to be a pleasant night.

<h1 style="text-align:center">2</h1>

Moreland woke up first. It took her a minute to remember where she was. When she did she turned to look at Jessica. She put a hand to Jessica's forehead. Still warm, but not burning up. At least, not yet.

Jessica stirred. Her eyes were slow to open.

Devon was already awake. He was staring out the front window at the ice.

"Anything wrong?" Moreland asked. At this point, she thought, it would make more sense just to assume there was some new dreadful problem waiting for them.

Devon shook his head. "No. Just trying to get a sense of what's ahead of us. It's easier see out here at dawn and dusk."

Jessica sat up. She looked around confused. "Damn. I was starting to reach for a piece of pizza."

"Why don't we get going." Moreland said looking at Devon.

Devon nodded and flipped the switch that started heating the diesel fuel. "We'll be ready in a few minutes."

"How do you feel?" Moreland asked Jessica.

"Tired still, I guess." Jessica said. "And pissed."

"Because you're sick?" Moreland asked.

Jessica shook her head. "No. That fucking pizza looked really good."

After a few minutes more Devon was able to get the LMTV started and they moved slowly off in the general direction of where the Main camp lay.

"Well, it ain't pizza, but it'll have to do." Jessica said fishing a sandwich out of what seemed to Moreland to be an endless number of pockets.

Jessica was in the process of going for a second bite of the sandwich when the whole LMTV lurched up at a steep angle. It slammed back down to the ground hard.

"Damn it, Scotty!" Jessica yelled.

"Sorry. I can't see some of these breaks in the ice." Devon said. He looked over at Jessica. She stared at him with the pink gray contents of the sandwich smeared across the right side of her face. He tried not laugh.

"Not fucking funny." Jessica said as she began wiping sandwich goo from her face.

They drove on for a couple more hours before they started to feel the engine shutter a little.

"What's that?" Moreland asked. "Is there something wrong with the engine?"

Devon shook his head. "No. We're running out of fuel."

They only went a little further before the LMTV engine shut down. All three sat in silence for a minute.

"Well, we should probably fire off a flare." Moreland said.

Devon nodded without saying anything.

"What's wrong?" Moreland asked.

Devon shrugged. "We're still quite a ways from the Main camp."

"I know." Moreland said. "But maybe they have sent some people out to check on the camp back there. If they do those people would be closer."

"Yeah." Devon said. "About that..."

"What?" Moreland asked.

"I'm not sure that we are still on the trail that leads back to the Main camp." Devon said.

"Oh." Moreland said.

"Without the road crew out here daily checking and clearing the trail it quickly gets lost in the blowing snow. I think we are in the general area though." Devon said.

"Well, they could still see the flare." Jessica said patting Devon on the arm.

Devon smiled at Jessica. He dug a flare and the flare gun out of a bag. He opened the door and leaned out. He fired off the flare and quickly pulled himself back into the LMTV.

For short time they just stared out at the ice stretching in all directions. It didn't take long for them to realize that this was going to be a long shot and, even if it worked, it could take a while.

Hours passed and the cold was steadily penetrating the cab of the LMTV. They were hunkered down under the blankets. As the afternoon wore on Devon tried sending up a couple more flares, but he was trying to be careful with their supply. They had a bag of flares to pull from, but Devon wanted to make sure they had some for the night. The flares would stand out better in dark of night.

"Great, just what we need." Moreland said. No one had spoken in over an hour. Her voice seemed almost jarring when the only sound they had been listening to was a faint whistle of wind trying to squeeze into the cab.

"What?" Jessica asked. Her head was beneath the blanket.

"A snow storm is coming." Moreland said.

Devon, whose head was only partially covered by blanket, stared out the front window. He was going to say something and then stopped.

"I don't think that's a snow storm." Devon said.

"Ah, wonderful. What now? Wait, let me guess. The whole Antarctic is breaking up and we are going to just drop into the ocean." Jessica said from under the blanket.

Moreland lifted the blanket up a little to look at Jessica. "You know that most of the ice in Antarctica is over land, right?"

Jessica shook her head. "Not with our luck."

Devon had reached over and grabbed a small set binoculars sitting on the dashboard of the vehicle. He scanned out to the distant swirling snow.

"I'll be damned." Devon said.

"What? What is it?" Moreland asked.

Jessica flipped the blanket off her head and sat up.

"Vehicles." Devon said.

"Quick. The flares." Moreland said.

"Right." Devon said. He grabbed the flare gun and a couple of flares. He leaned out of the cab and shot both flares.

"Hand him more." Moreland said to Jessica.

Jessica grabbed more and started feeding Devon flares.

"What the hell?" Jessica said staring out the window. "They're gone."

Moreland studied the horizon too. The swirling snow had disappeared. "Shit."

Devon ducked back into the LMTV. He was smiling. "They stopped." Devon looked through the binoculars again.

"What's happening?" Moreland asked, but she had hardly finished her question when the swirling snow started again.

"They're coming." Devon said.

"Oh, my God." Moreland said obviously relieved. "I didn't think we had a chance in hell of this working."

"Really?" Jessica said. "Cause, you know, my life is hanging in the balance here."

Moreland shrugged. "Well, I couldn't think of anything better."

It took a while for the vehicles to draw near them. There were six vehicles. They looked similar to the LMTV they were in, but these were clearly meant for other kinds of duty. Three of them were armed with 50 caliber machine guns on top.

The vehicles stopped twenty yards in front of them. About a half dozen soldiers climbed out pointing guns at them. In addition, the three bigger guns were quickly manned by soldiers.

"I am so happy to see them." Jessica said.

Devon and Moreland each pushed their doors open and started stepping out of the cab. In an instant, guns began firing. Some of the bullets clanged off the LMTV. Moreland Devon ducked back into the cab.

"What the fuck?" Moreland said. "What are they doing?"

"Trying to kill us." Jessica yelled. "They're fucking zombie soldiers."

"Son of a bitch! Can't get away from these damned things?" Moreland said.

Devon was peeking up over the dashboard. He watched the soldiers. "I don't think these are zombies. They don't act like the ones we ran into."

"Well, then why in the hell are they trying to kill us?" Moreland asked.

"Because," Devon thought for a moment, "they think we are the zombies."

The soldiers were slowly, carefully drawing closer.

"Oh, for Christ's sake." Moreland said. She was pissed. She flipped the lever on the window next to her and shoved the window open.

"Stop fucking shooting at us you morons! We're not fucking zombies!" Moreland yelled out the window.

"Nice." Jessica said with a nod.

The effect on the soldiers was immediate. They stopped moving and stood staring at the LMTV. It seemed like their guns lower a little as well.

From directly in front of their vehicle one soldier, unarmed, walked through the line of armed soldiers and approached Moreland's side of the LMTV.

"Doctor Moreland?"

Moreland leaned cautiously out the window a little as the soldier pulled his hood back. "Major Wilkins?"

"Well, I'll be damned." Wilkins said.

Moreland started opening the door to get out again.

Wilkins held up a hand. "Wait."

Moreland stopped and watched him. Wilkins turned and waved towards the other vehicles. It took a couple of minutes, but three soldiers came from the back of one of the vehicles. They were carrying hazmat suits.

"You need to put these on." Wilkins said. The soldiers laid the suits down and backed away as did Wilkins.

Moreland, Jessica and Devon climbed down from the LMTV. They started working their way into the suits.

"Who the hell were these made for?" Jessica asked. "I think two people could share one of these."

Once they were in the suits one soldier who was also in a hazmat suit came over and made sure they were sealed up properly.

Wilkins then moved up next to Moreland. "I swear to God I thought all of you people from in the Trench were lost."

"It was...a journey." Moreland said through the suit. She was surprised at how much emotion seemed to sweep over her. The thought that maybe this whole thing was over. Then a thought came to her.

"The Main camp...is it OK?" Moreland asked.

Wilkins nodded. "The Main camp is secure. We were just coming out to see if there were any survivors from the upper camp."

Moreland shook her head. "We didn't see any. Just...the infected ones."

Wilkins face looked strained and sad. He nodded. "OK. Let's get you guys back to the Main camp."

The drive back to the Main camp took hours. They said very little on the ride. The suits made it hard to talk to one another. Moreland was fine with that. She lowered her head so no one could see into the face shield and quietly cried.

3

Moreland sat in the room and waited. It had been a while and she was getting tired of staring at the same four walls. There were two folding chairs and a folding table in the room and nothing else. She knew they were being very cautious, but she was beginning to feel like she was a prisoner.

Finally someone came to the door and unlocked it. When the man came in Moreland was happy that this time he was not wearing a hazmat suit. He pulled out the other chair and sat down. He was tall with silver hair and a very weary look in his eyes.

"My name is Major Mason. I am the doctor here." Mason said. "You seem to belong to our special club."

"Your club?" Moreland asked.

"A small minority seem to be able to fend off the virus." Mason said. "For whatever reason, the virus doesn't seem to like you much."

"It's probably the sarcasm. It annoys everyone." Moreland said.

Mason gave a slight nod. "Perhaps." Mason was going to say something else when someone opened the door. It was Wilkins. He stepped in and leaned against the wall.

"I am sure you have quite a story to tell." Wilkins said.

Moreland nodded. "It's definitely the most eventful dig I've ever been on."

"Right. Well, I would like to hear your story, but our doctor here," Wilkins waved towards Mason, "feels we are under a bit of hurry to sort this virus problem out."

Moreland nodded again and looked at Mason.

"I have been trying isolate the virus, but it has been somewhat frustrating. It seems to have the ability to mutate at a rapid rate. It would greatly help our cause if I could find ground zero for this virus. The first person that had it. With most, if not all, of the people in the Trench now likely dead that may prove to be impossible. Finding someone very near the beginning of the chain would allow me a look at this thing before it has spun through so many others mutating along the way. So, my long shot is hoping like hell you have any idea who was one of the first people in the Trench that exhibited symptoms." Mason said.

Moreland shook her head slightly. "I have no idea who were the first ones to get sick. There were numerous people showing signs of being sick. They just thought it was a cold."

Mason nodded. "Damn. And yes it starts out like a cold, until it works its way into the brain and then the fever starts. Eventually, as you have seen first hand, the person seems to lose all sense of reason and, oddly, all of them seem to turn violent."

A thought occurred to Moreland and she looked sharply at Mason. "Jessica."

Mason held up a hand. "I know. I have given her a shot of a concoction I have come up with that boosts the immune system. It seems to significantly slow down the virus if it hasn't progressed too far. She should be OK. For now. It's not a cure. It just buys us time. We really need to get back as close as we can to person zero to come up with something that will beat it."

As if on cue the door swung open and Jessica and Devon appeared. They smiled at Moreland.

"How are you feeling?" Moreland asked Jessica.

"Better. Kind of like being hungover." Jessica said.

"Ah, well, something you're familiar with anyway." Moreland said.

Jessica was about to object and then thought for a moment. "OK. Yeah, maybe."

Moreland turned and gave Mason a quizzical look. "Wait, I don't understand. If you want the virus in its original form why don't you go to the source?"

Mason's eyes narrowed. "You know the source?"

Moreland nodded. "Yeah. It's a virus that has laid dormant in the soil were our dig site is."

"And you know this, how?" Mason asked.

"The Morrosaurus." Moreland said.

"The what?" Mason asked.

"The Moronasaurus." Jessica says. "They were killing each other. I was right. Look at me." Jessica pointed a thumb back at herself. "Ice climbing queen and fucking paleontological genius."

Moreland sighed. "Morrosaurus. For now let's just stick with ice climbing and sandwiches."

"Hey, you know that's really not very—-actually," Jessica looked at Devon, "I am kind of hungry."

"The Morrosaurus are herbivores. The fossil scene we were uncovering in the Trench was depicting them in what could only be explained as large numbers of the specimens apparently killing each other. That is very definitely not their expected behavior. This virus affected them the same way it is affecting humans." Moreland said.

Mason shook his head slowly. "I've...never seen any virus that could manipulate its host. Not like what you are suggesting."

"Well, that's what we were seeing in the fossils. Regardless, that virus was in the soil. I am certain it's there." Moreland said.

"That's a long time for a virus to lie dormant and still be viable." Mason said skeptically.

"But not impossible." Moreland replied.

Mason sighed. "No. Not impossible."

"So, if what the doctor says is true and, for the record, I believe she is correct, then if you want the virus in its original form we need to go back down there and get some soil samples for you, correct?" Wilkins asked looking at Mason.

Mason nodded slowly. "I guess so."

"I ain't going back there." Jessica said.

"I will take some men back down there and get what we need." Wilkins said.

"I'll go too." Moreland said.

"There's no need for you to go back there." Wilkins said.

"There's a lot of soil down there and we have no idea where this virus might be. You could collect a hundred soil samples down there and still not hit a spot that contained the virus. That makes it something of a crap shoot and it doesn't sound like we have the time to guess where the virus is. If I'm right and the Morrosaurus did have this virus then we need to get soil samples from our dig site and some of the fossils themselves." Moreland said.

"She's right." Mason said.

Wilkins and Mason exchanged a look.

"What?" Moreland asked.

Wilkins shook his head. "It is nothing really. We...haven't quite worked out the command structure here yet."

"What do you mean?" Moreland asked.

Mason sighed. He seemed mildly annoyed at the current discussion. "Colonel Evans was in McMurdo when this started. He is the commanding officer here."

"Major Mason feels like command would automatically default to him. He is, however, a doctor and I am a field officer." Wilkins said.

"This really doesn't seem like the time to go through this." Moreland said.

Mason nodded.

"Probably not." Wilkins said. He looked at Mason. "OK, well, we're burning daylight. I'll get the men refueling the vehicles."

Mason nodded again.

Wilkins looked at Moreland. "How much time do you need to rest and be ready?"

Moreland glanced at Jessica. Knowing that Jessica was fighting off the virus worried her. It was more than that. It haunted her. She looked back at Wilkins. "As soon as you and your men are ready we can go."

Wilkins stared at Moreland for just a moment with the trace of a smile. He gave a slight shake of his head. "OK, Doc."

It didn't take long for Wilkins and his men to get prepped to head back out. Moreland used the time to eat part of sandwich that she was thankful did not emerge from one of Jessica's pockets, somewhat smashed. She slammed down a can of some kind of energy drink and then joined Wilkins in the cab of one of their modified LMTVs.

Moreland sat between Wilkins and the soldier driving the LMTV. More soldiers were in the back. They headed out in the mid afternoon. The long summer days of the Antarctic still afforded them many more hours of daylight. They rode in silence of a while.

Finally Moreland turned to look at Wilkins. "OK. I have to ask. What was the deal with the Bible on your desk?"

Wilkins thought for a moment. He seemed unsure if he wanted to answer her question. Then he just gave a small shrug.

"I was raised in Alabama. Pretty strict Baptists. For them, the answer for everything was in the Bible. I don't know that I ever really bought into any of that. I'll tell you what, though, watching my men indiscriminately killing one another...I don't know. I never experienced anything like that before. Didn't understand what I was seeing. There seemed to be nothing I could do to stop it. I guess...hell, I don't know, I think it just brought a lot of that old stuff back out. If you were going to imagine what the 'End of Times' might look like, well, that would be my guess." Wilkins sighed when he finished. He stared straight ahead out the front window.

Moreland nodded. "OK. I get that, but I'm not convinced we've reached any 'End of Times' just yet. We survived COVID, I think can find a way to beat this."

Wilkins shook his head a little. "I don't share your optimism. I lost my brother and his youngest girl to COVID. I think humanity is more vulnerable now than ever. I think COVID only made us weaker. It showed how self destructive we can be. So many people simply refused to believe it was real or they refused to adhere any kind of protocol that would help to contain it or save the lives of their fellow humans. It was just crazy stupid. And the fact that we survived only made those people believe they were right in pretending it wasn't a real danger. Surviving it just made people less fearful of a pandemic now. You unleash a virus like this one on them and I think it's game over. This is more contagious. This is lethal in almost one 100% of the infections and, even worse, it turns us against ourselves."

Moreland hesitated. She was, in fact, a little embarrassed. "Honestly, I'm not that optimistic. I said that because maybe I wanted to hear it. Because I wanted someone to say that to me. To assure me that we would overcome something like this. Obviously, that's not you."

Wilkins looked at Moreland. He gave her a small smile. "Sorry. I've never been very good at sugar coating things. Comes from listening to too many Old Testament stories."

Moreland was quiet. She was staring down at the floor. Finally, she lifted her head and looked Wilkins in the eye.

"When we were at the upper camp...and it seemed like everyone else was dead...and I knew we were probably carrying it...this virus that was killing everybody...we, well, I suggested that...we should...to try to stop it..." Moreland said slowly. She couldn't finish it.

Wilkins nodded slowly. It was apparent he knew what she was trying to admit to. He studied Moreland's face for a moment. "You are one gutsy scientist."

4

"A fork?" The soldier asked.

"You bet your ass. A fork. Hung there from it." Jessica said.

Devon walked into the infirmary. Jessica smiled waving him over.

"I was telling Jason here about—-" Jessica started to explain.

"I heard." Devon said.

"Oh, right. Well, tell him it's true." Jessica said.

Devon glanced over at the soldier. He nodded. "Yeah. It actually happened."

"It was pretty damned cool." Jessica said. "You aren't making it sound as cool as it was."

Devon looked at Jessica. "It wasn't cool at the time. It was scary as hell."

Jessica could tell Devon wasn't going to be excited about the incident. "Oh, well, yeah, it was kind of scary, I guess. Anyway, do you two know each other?"

Devon glanced at the soldier and shook his head.

"Jason Wells." Wells held his hand out.

Devon stepped around the bed Jessica was sitting on and shook Wells' hand. "Scott Devon."

"Jason got the shot I got. For the virus. The boostery thing." Jessica said.

"And you're doing OK?" Devon asked.

"So far. I was feeling pretty shitty before the Doc gave me it. Been doing better. It kind of comes and goes." Wells said.

"Well, that's good to hear." Devon said.

Mason walked into the infirmary. He stopped next to Jessica's bed. He felt her forehead and back of her neck. He pulled out a thermometer and checked her temperature.

"Low grade, but no different. That's good." Mason said. He stepped around and did the same for Wells. He did Wells a second time.

"Up a little, but not significantly. We'll take that as good sign as well." Mason said.

"So...you think we're going to be OK?" Jessica asked.

Mason nodded slightly. "I think if I can get a good look at the original form of the virus I can find something to keep it at bay."

"Did they say how long it would take them to get out there and get your samples?" Jessica asked.

Mason shrugged. "Hard to say. They know the importance of what they're doing so I am sure they will be as quick as they can. Barring any trouble, we could see them back before morning."

"We had nothing but trouble out there." Jessica said. She looked up at Devon standing next to her. He nodded.

"Well, Major Wilkins and his men know what they are up against now so I am certain they can handle this. In the meantime, I am working on an even stronger booster. From your doctor Moreland and this young man," Mason patted Devon on the shoulder, "we have two more samples of people that have shown a stronger T-cell reaction to this thing."

"T-cell?" Jessica asked.

"They are the big guns of your immune system. They do most of the ass-kicking when it comes to fighting off infections. Some people have stronger T-cell responses than others." Mason explained.

Jessica elbowed Devon in the hip. "Lucky bastard."

Devon smiled. "Good clean living."

"Huh, well, I can fix that." Jessica said.

There was a loud crack. A gun shot. For a moment everyone froze. Mason and Wells seemed puzzled, but Devon and Jessica looked alarmed.

Two more shots followed.

"I'll see what's going on." Devon said. He pulled out his M18 and walked out of the infirmary.

"It's probably nothing." Mason said.

Jessica shook her head. "Around here, it's never nothing."

5

The LMTVs slowed as they approached the upper camp. There seemed to be no movement. No activity. Wilkins ordered the vehicles to park around the crane.

"We'll wait here for a few minutes." Wilkins told Moreland as they stood next the LMTV. In front of them was the crane and beyond that the edge of the Trench. Behind them a group of soldiers scouted the immediate area for any trouble.

While they waited a couple more soldiers began checking out the crane and preparing it for operation. She harbored a fear that the crane was unusable, for some reason, and they would need to repel down into the Trench. She didn't think she was up to that. Plus the added time it would take to do that would mean it was more time before they got back and Mason could come up with something to save Jessica.

A soldier circled around the LMTV and approached Wilkins. "Nothing, sir."

Wilkins nodded. "Keep a couple of guys posted over there and the rest of you can start setting up the satellite link."

"Yes, sir." The soldier turned and disappeared behind the LMTV.

Moreland glanced at Wilkins and then walked slowly over towards the crane. Wilkins joined her.

"You OK, Doc?" Wilkins asked.

Moreland nodded. "Are they going to be able to get this thing working?"

Wilkins turned and yelled something over to the soldiers on the crane. They signaled back to him. He turned back to Moreland.

"They say they'll be ready in a few minutes." Wilkins said.

"Yeah, well, I've done about all the climbing I have in me." Moreland said.

Wilkins smiled. "Yeah, that was a pretty impressive feat. Anyway, worst case, the boys here could use the winches on the vehicles to lower us down."

"I wouldn't be too excited about that, but it's getting back up that would worry me more." Moreland said.

"Not to worry. My guys would get us back up." Wilkins said.

"If they are still here and able to." Moreland said. She glanced around at the remnants of the upper camp.

Wilkins followed her gaze and then shook his head. "Don't you worry about that." Wilkins pointed up at the top of the LMTVs. "Those 50 calibers will drive any trouble away."

The sound of the crane's diesel engine rumbled to life. Wilkins and Moreland watched as the crane began to slowly crank the platform up from below. It didn't take too long before the platform appeared up over the edge.

Wilkins and Moreland backed away to stay clear of where the platform was being set down. Once the platform was settled on the ice the engine of the crane eased back down to an idle.

Wilkins walked over and went through some things with the soldiers on the crane and then turned to talk to several other soldiers who immediately began gathering their gear. Wilkins walked back over to Moreland. He was about say something to her when another soldier came running over to him.

"Sir?" The soldier said at Wilkins shoulder.

Wilkins turned. "What is it?"

"Communications are up. And...when we checked in with the Main camp they told us they have some issues there." The soldier said.

"What issues?" Wilkins asked.

"Not sure. They weren't sure the extent yet. Something about the virus thing having gotten out among the boys there." The soldier said.

"Shit." Moreland said from behind Wilkins.

"Damn it." Wilkins sighed. "OK. Tell them we are going for the samples right now. We will be back ASAP. Understood?"

"Yes, sir." The soldier turned and dashed off.

Three more soldiers walked over to Wilkins. They were sporting XM7 rifles and small packs on their backs. Wilkins gave them a sign to wait.

Wilkins turned around to look at Moreland. "Are you ready?"

"I guess, but I think I would feel better if I had one of those." Moreland said pointing at Wilkins' holstered M18.

Wilkins glanced down at his sidearm. He looked at Moreland for a moment and then turned around.

Wilkins waved a hand at one of the soldiers. "Give me your sidearm." The soldier complied.

Wilkins turned and handed it to Moreland with a small smile. "We'll make a soldier out of you yet."

Moreland shook her head. "No. I'm too scared." She tucked the gun into her waist.

"If you weren't scared, you'd be useless as a soldier. Fear is just another tool in your toolbox. You use it when you need it." Wilkins said.

"My toolbox is plenty full of that right now." A soldier from behind Wilkins said.

Wilkins smiled at Moreland. He turned and waved at the soldiers behind him. "Let's go."

Wilkins, Moreland and the three soldiers walked on to the platform. They anchored themselves to the platform with a strap and Wilkins gave the signal to the guys operating the crane. Slowly the platform lifted up and the crane rotated around. For a moment the platform just hung over the edge of the Trench. Two soldiers hung on to the cables keeping the platform from spinning. Then the platform started descending.

As the platform sunk into the fog Moreland looked down at the floor of the platform. She thought about Palfrey, Beecham and the others she watched die down there. A shiver ran through her. A voice in her head spoke to her: What the hell were you thinking coming back here?

6

When the platform thumped down on to the ground in the Trench, Moreland was ready for it this time. She had braced herself. Out of the corner of her eye she saw two of the soldiers knocked sideways from a kneeling position and hit the floor of the platform awkwardly. They cursed as they stood up. Moreland smiled slightly. Rookies.

Moreland unhooked the strap to the platform floor and slowly walked off the platform. Wilkins watched her hesitation at stepping off the platform. He stepped over to her.

"You OK?" Wilkins asked.

Moreland glanced over at him. "I'll admit I'm having a little PTSD."

Wilkins gave a quick nod. "That's understandable. Let me assure you that you'll be fine. These men here know what we are dealing with. Besides, it's likely that everyone down here, by now, is dead."

Moreland took a deep breath. "I know. Let's go."

They started walking into the fog.

"You sure you can get us to the camp?" Moreland asked. "All the markers are gone."

Wilkins nodded. "I spent time down here after it was initially cleared helping with the layout. I'll get us there."

They walked for a little while and Moreland was sure that Wilkins had missed the camp and was leading them off into a foggy nowhere. She was almost right. Just to their right one of the soldiers thought he saw a shape in the fog. They veered right and discovered they had almost walked past the camp. They were at the opposite side from where the Admin tent was located.

Moreland was fine with that. She had no desire to walk back into the Admin tent. The sight of Laurence and the all the blood would haunt her.

They walked only a short distance into that end of the camp. Nothing was stirring. They could just make out a few bodies on the boundary of their vision. Wilkins turned and looked at Moreland.

"I guess from here you are our guide." Wilkins said.

Moreland nodded. She walked a little further into the camp. She was trying to recognize the tents that they walked between to find the path out to the dig site. It was difficult since many of the tents had been wrecked in some fashion. Finally she went with her best guess.

They walked towards the gap between a couple of tents. Moreland glanced quickly to her right. She was pretty sure they were only one tent away from where the young girl had been stabbed. She pushed that image out of her head and passed between the tents. Wilkins and his men followed her.

At first she was afraid she too would lead them off into the fog and what seemed like oblivion. She thought the ground at their feet looked worn like the path to the dig site had been, but she wasn't sure. Thankfully, after a few more steps an intact marker emerged from the fog. She oriented herself based on that marker and kept going.

Clearly there were other markers missing, but she pushed on. A second marker appeared to her right and she again adjusted their direction slightly. Another few minutes and there it was. The dig site. Just as they had left it.

"Nice work." Wilkins said with a smile.

"Thanks." Moreland said.

"So what specifically are we looking for?" Wilkins asked. He gestured to one of the soldiers. The soldier flipped his pack off and produced some small containers.

Moreland took a step forward and started to point when a loud banging sound came from somewhere behind them. All four of them spun around. They saw nothing but fog.

"That sounded like it was from the camp." Moreland said.

Wilkins nodded his head slightly. "Yeah."

They listened for another minute. It seemed like a second sound came from that direction as well, but it was muffled and difficult to be sure if it was real or not.

Wilkins pointed at two of the soldiers. "You two, go check on that. Stay on comms." Wilkins pointed to the walkie-talkies they had on their belts. They nodded and started to turn back the way they had come.

"Hey." Wilkins said. The two soldiers looked back at him. "Stay in sight of each other. Got it?"

"Yes, sir." They both answered. They turned and disappeared into the fog.

"Are you sure that's a good idea?" Moreland asked.

Wilkins nodded. "They'll be fine. And we can handle things here." He waved at the remaining soldier and himself.

Moreland looked at Wilkins. He could tell she was nervous.

"Let's get what we came for and get out. Show me where we should get this dirt from." Wilkins said.

Moreland nodded. She turned and pointed out the three dig sites. "We need soil samples from each of those spots. Right around where the fossils are. I'm going to pull some fossils out and bag those up."

Wilkins took a couple of the containers. He unscrewed the lid from one of them.

"I'm no scientist, Doc. Is there anything special I need to know about collecting this dirt?" Wilkins asked.

"Yeah. The dirt goes on the inside of the bottle." Moreland said.

Wilkins looked at her. "You do that sarcasm thing a lot, don't you?"

Moreland shrugged. "Yeah. I guess so. Just comes natural."

"It's pretty damned annoying." Wilkins said.

"Yeah and I'm still single. Go figure." Moreland said with a slight smile.

"Right." Wilkins said and headed over towards one of the dig sites.

Wilkins had walked a few steps away when there gun shots coming from the direction of the camp. Wilkins turned to look back towards the camp. He glanced at Moreland. She was looking at him.

"They are just clearing the area of anything. If there was a problem they would be calling me." Wilkins said.

Moreland sighed. "I don't want to go down that road again."

Wilkins held up a hand. "It's OK. We'll be OK."

Moreland looked back in the direction of the camp. She looked back at Wilkins. He nodded at her.

Slowly Moreland turned and made herself kneel down at the fossils she had been working on. It was an effort to focus because with each passing minute she had a growing feeling that one of those infected soldiers was running up behind her.

"What's our status?" Mason asked the soldier.

"The building is secured, sir." The soldier answer.

"All doors and windows?" Mason asked.

"Yes sir." The soldier replied. It was obvious that he wanted to say something, but hesitated.

Mason saw it. "What is it?"

"Is...it true that the other two camps...that everyone there is dead?" The soldier asked.

Mason took a deep breath and let it out slowly. "I don't know the answer to that question, soldier. What's your name?"

"Eddie Colten. Private Colten, sir." Colten replied.

"OK, Private Colten, do you know how many soldiers outside of this building are infected?" Mason asked.

Colten shook his head. "I...don't know how many. It's kind of hard to tell who is and who isn't."

"How do you know that you are not infected?" Mason asked.

Colten started to say something and then stopped. "I..."

Mason stepped closer to Colten and put a hand on his forehead. "I don't feel a fever, at least, not a significant one. So, what that means is if you are infected you are not on the verge of becoming violent. Understood?"

Colten felt his own forehead. "OK. Did you want me to go check the foreheads of the guys outside?"

Mason looked at Colten for a few seconds. "No, son, I do not. I was just explaining a cursory way in which you can test if someone is infected and close to losing control. That's all. As far as how many out there are infected I wasn't looking for an exact number. I just wanted a sense of whether it appeared to be a lot of feverish and violent soldiers out there or a few."

Colten nodded. "Yes sir. There were some, but not the whole camp."

Mason was standing in the doorway to the infirmary as he talked to Colten. "How many soldiers do we have on the inside of the building?"

"Three. Counting myself, sir." Colten answered.

"I can help." Wells said sliding off the edge of the bed.

Mason looked back at Wells and nodded. "OK."

"Then we have five." Devon said as he stood next the bed Jessica sat on. He held up his M18.

"OK." Mason said. "I want only one accessible way into or out of this building."

"OK. That would be the door that Sergeant Taylor ordered us through. He sent us in and told us not to open it for anyone." Colten said.

"Perfect." Mason said. "And what was Sergeant Taylor's plan for outside of the building?"

"He intends to kill everyone that exhibits any signs of the virus." Colten said.

"Damn it. That's going to be a blood bath." Mason was clearly frustrated by something, but he didn't explain what. After a moment he looked at Colten again.

"Take Wells and Devon here and double check the barricades on every entry point in this building. Then I want one man on the one door we use for entry all the time. Got it?" Mason said.

Colten nodded. "Yes, sir." He glanced over at Devon and Wells who both moved to join him in the doorway.

Jessica slid off the bed and started to follow Devon, but Mason stopped her.

"You stay here." Mason said.

"I can help them." Jessica said. "Didn't they tell you? I'm kind of a bad ass now."

"Wonderful. I'm happy for you, but you are going to help prep the lab for when Wilkins and Moreland return. I'm afraid the clock is ticking now." Mason said.

"You mean for me?" Jessica asked.

"I mean for all of us." Mason said.

Jessica was going to say something, but gun fire erupted from somewhere outside the building. By the sound of it, it was close.

Jessica and Mason exchanged a look.

"Let's get to work." Mason said and headed for the lab. Jessica followed.

8

Moreland worked as quickly as she could. She kept glancing over at Wilkins as he collected a couple of soil samples. He kept looking back towards the camp. Clearly it bothered him that he had not heard from his soldiers.

Finally Wilkins stood and stared into the fog. He grabbed the mic of his walkie-talkie. "This Wilkins. Report. What's going on in the camp?"

Moreland stood up and looked over at Wilkins.

"Damn it." Wilkins said quietly. He talked into the mic again. "This is Wilkins. Report."

Moreland and Wilkins exchanged a serious look.

There was crackling on the walkie-talkie and then a voice. "...they're all over the place..." There was more crackling and they heard another gun shot. "...only look dead..."

"Shit." Moreland said.

"Damn it." Wilkins said. He looked at Moreland. "We need to get going."

Moreland nodded. "Yeah."

Wilkins walked over to Moreland and held up the two containers he had of soil. "Is this enough?"

"It'll have to be. I've got a few fossil pieces. Should be enough for Mason to get a look at this thing." Moreland said. "Maybe I'll grab one piece from Laurence's site."

Moreland walked a little further out to where Palfrey had been digging. She knelt down and began wiggling a vertebrae out of the soil. She heard a scuffling sound to her right. She assumed it was Wilkins walking up next to her. She turned and saw a shape moving towards her out of the fog. Her head spun around quickly and saw that Wilkins had walked over and was talking to the remaining soldier still with them.

Moreland twisted back around. The shape formed into a ragged and clearly wounded soldier. He carried an automatic rifle and seemed to be trying to lift it up in her direction.

"Shit. Shit." Moreland said. She wrestled the gun out of her waist and swung it towards the soldier.

From behind her she heard Wilkins voice. "Doc, get down. You're in the line of fire."

The infected soldier squeezed the trigger and started firing off rounds. To Moreland's right the ground started churning and dust swirled next to her.

Moreland started firing at the soldier. She wasn't sure how many shots she fired and didn't care. She just kept firing. She saw the soldier's body jerked back a couple of times and then he fell backwards.

A moment later Wilkins was next to her. He stepped over to the dead soldier and then turned back to Moreland.

"Good job." Wilkins said, putting a hand on her shoulder.

Moreland looked up at Wilkins. "Yeah, well, if I don't make it out of here tell Jessica I hit something with this," she held up the gun, "and she can kiss my smashed turtle ass."

Wilkins looked at for a moment. "OK. That's the strangest epithet I've ever heard."

Moreland shrugged.

Wilkins helped her to her feet. "Let's get going."

"Yeah." Moreland said. "I think we've worn out our welcome here."

9

The gun fire grew louder. Jessica thought it was just outside of the building they were in. She was helping Mason lay out test tubes and bottles and prep a couple of tables. She got the impression he wasn't thrilled with her work.

"You've actually washed dishes before, right?" Mason asked.

Jessica hesitated. It sounded like a trick question. I mean, she thought, who washes dishes anymore?

"I...have a dishwasher." Jessica said.

Mason sighed. "Well, that explains a lot. These flasks have to be sterile."

"Yeah. I was cleaning them up." Jessica said.

"You blew into one." Mason said.

"It looked dusty." Jessica said.

Mason sighed. He stepped over to a table and picked up a piece of paper. He handed the paper to her.

"This is a list of items we need from the supply cabinet out in the hallway. Gather them up and bring them in here." Mason said.

Jessica glanced at the doorway and back at Mason. "There are a bunch of cabinets out there. How do I know which one is the supply cabinet?"

Mason stared at her. "The one labeled 'Supply Cabinet.'"

Jessica nodded once. "Right. I'm on it."

Jessica went out into the hall. She found the supply cabinet and began gathering things from the list. The gun fire outside was sporadic and it made her jittery. She got everything on the list that she could identify and carried it back into the lab.

Mason turned as she came in. He watched her deposit the items on to a table. He stepped over to her and laid a hand on her forehead.

"Let's check your temperature." Mason said.

"Do I feel hot?" Jessica asked.

"No." Mason said retrieving a thermometer.

"I had a boy tell me I was hot once." Jessica said. "Of course, he was kind of drunk at this party and so, you know, it probably doesn't count for much." Jessica said.

Mason looked at Jessica with no expression at all. "I have absolutely nothing to say regarding that." He glanced at the thermometer and nodded. "OK."

Jessica was going to say something when Devon came into the lab.

"Private Wells and Private Colten are standing watch at the main door. I have been cycling through the rest of the building verifying our barricades are holding." Devon said.

Mason nodded. "Good. The moment you here from Sergeant Taylor, specifically if he has gained complete control of the camp, I want to know."

"Yes sir." Devon said. "I'll relay that to Wells and Colten." Devon glanced at Jessica and then headed back out into the hall.

Some more shots rang out and then a moment later the lights went out. Seconds passed and then red emergency lights came on. It gave everything an odd and eerie look.

"Shit." Jessica said.

"Hmm, that doesn't seem like a good sign." Mason said.

It was quiet in the lab for a few minutes. Mason was going over the equipment he had set out and seemed satisfied with it.

"What happens...if you can't find a cure for this thing?" Jessica asked.

Mason glanced over at her. "If it comes to that, I guess we will have to make some decisions."

"When we were at the upper camp...and we thought we were the only ones left...Dr. Moreland said we had to consider killing ourselves in order to make sure it didn't get out to the rest of the world." Jessica said. Her voice was a little quieter than usual. "Is that what you meant?"

Mason turned to look at her. He sighed. "The Army spends a great deal of time and tax payer money scoping out contingencies for every possible disaster scenario."

"Who makes contingencies for a prehistoric virus popping up and turning people into crazed killers?" Jessica asked.

"Well, maybe not this exact scenario, but you'd be surprised at all the things we plan for. Some of them even more crazy than this. Anyway, there are sufficient protocols in place that would adequately overlap to cover this." Mason said.

"So...what is the plan for this scenario?" Jessica asked.

Mason shrugged. "Probably one of the basic ones. Nuke the site."

"The dig site?" Jessica asked.

Mason shook his head. "All of it. All three camps."

"Us too?" Jessica asked. Her voice carried a level of panic to it.

Mason nodded.

"That's crazy." Jessica said.

"Have to make sure everyone else is safe. Besides, we have a lot of extra nukes laying around we don't have any other use for." Mason said with a brief smile.

"Not funny." Jessica said. She hoped he was joking about the nukes, but he didn't seem like the joking kind of military guy. A moment later she wondered if any military guys had a sense of humor.

"I am confident it won't come to that. We are pretty isolated down here so there is likely to be other options on the table as well." Mason said.

"Does it involve us living through this?" Jessica asked.

Mason shrugged. "Let's say it does."

"That doesn't sound very comforting." Jessica said.

"We're the Army, comforting is not really our thing. We're more big picture." Mason said. "Now, let's go through what you have gathered and see what we might still be missing."

10

They moved through the fog cautiously. Wilkins was on Moreland's right and the remaining soldier still with them moved on her left. All three held their guns ready. Moreland kept looking back over her shoulder. She couldn't shake a feeling that something was going to suddenly jump at her from behind.

They had heard a couple more shots when they first started back towards the lower camp, but nothing since. Wilkins had tried to contact his men, but received no reply. They moved slowly and minutes dragged by. They did their best to follow their scuffled tracks in the dirt back to the camp. After a short while they were rewarded with the bulky shape of the backside of a tent looming before them in the fog.

Wilkins held up a hand. He gestured for them to be quiet. He took a moment to make sure both Moreland and the soldier made eye contact with him. Then he went through a couple of motions. It was clear he wanted Moreland to lag a couple of steps behind himself and the soldier. Moreland nodded her understanding.

Easing forward they crept between two tents. The quiet was almost more frightening than if there were guns firing. The soldier now was in front. He peeked out around the front corner of the tent and then turned to Wilkins indicating he didn't see anything. Wilkins waved him forward.

The three of them stepped out into the open center of the camp. They could still see bodies laying around, but they were gray shapes. They knew the shapes were the dead bodies of fallen comrades, but in the fog they had dissolved into undefined objects.

It happened fast. The cracking sound. The flashes in the swirling mist. The soldier in front of Wilkins crying out and falling.

"Get back!" He yelled at Moreland over his shoulder. He fired twice towards the flashes and grabbed the soldier, now laying on the ground, and dragged him backwards.

Moreland scrambled back between two tents stumbling over something and falling. Wilkins was there a moment later and tripped over Moreland's legs pulling the soldier partly on top of himself. Wilkins and Moreland dragged themselves up on to their knees.

"Check on him." Wilkins said to Moreland indicating the wounded soldier. She nodded.

Wilkins eased up to the corner of the tent. He peeked around it. He saw nothing moving. No sounds. No stirring.

"He's bleeding bad." Moreland said.

Wilkins eased back to the other side of the soldier. "How bad?"

"I'm no medic, but I can tell you we need to tie this off." Moreland waved a hand at the blood streaming out of the soldier's upper thigh.

"Damn it." Wilkins said. He hesitated for just a second and then quickly unlaced one of the soldier's boots. He handed the lace to Moreland.

Moreland stared at the lace and then at Wilkins.

Wilkins nodded at Moreland. "I'll lift his leg. You get that around it."

Moreland didn't move. She was lost for the moment revisiting the Admin tent and Palfrey's body.

"Now." Wilkins said firmly.

Moreland shook herself, sucked in a breath and nodded. She adjusted the lace in her hands and then nodded at Wilkins. He lifted the leg. Blood ran all over his leg, their hands, the dirt all around.

Moreland jammed the lace under the leg and pulled it through. She pulled the ends up and tried to start a knot. The lace was slippery with blood and she was struggling with it. She was almost panicking now. Wilkins put a hand on her wrist and looked her in the eye. He nodded reassuringly.

Wilkins lowered the leg and helped Moreland get the lace tied as tightly as they could. Blood still oozed out of the wound. Moreland

and Wilkins looked at one another. It was obviously they needed to do more than this for him.

"Bandages." Moreland said softly. She was afraid to speak because there was still someone out there with the intention of killing them.

Wilkins nodded. He looked around, but there was nothing laying around on the ground between two tents that was going to help them. He pulled his knife and, catching Moreland's eye, indicated what he was going to do. Moreland nodded.

Wilkins slid over close to the nearest tent and cut a lengthy slice down the side. He peeked through the slit. He glanced at Moreland and gestured that he was going inside the tent. A moment later he was out of sight.

Moreland sat for a couple of seconds and then a wave of panic swept through her. She realized that somewhere in helping the soldier she no longer had the gun in her hand. She clawed around at her waist. She felt it right away. Somehow she had, without thinking, tucked the gun away. She pulled the gun back out and waited.

Minutes passed. Moreland started getting worried. What was taking Wilkins so long? A new wave of panic now shook her. What happens if Wilkins gets killed? How would she get out of this camp alive? What if the soldiers up top had been killed? How would she get back up to the top? She knew she couldn't climb back up the ice wall by herself and...

The soft sound of Wilkins reemerging from the tent broke off Moreland's train of thought. She sighed heavily. She didn't realize she had been holding breath for the last minute.

Wilkins held up a piece of clothing. The two of them turned their attention back the wounded soldier and came to the same realization. The soldier was already dead. Wilkins threw the piece of clothing away. He knelt next to the body staring down.

Moreland put a hand on his shoulder. Wilkins didn't look up. He just shook his head.

"I am sick to death of watching my men die." Wilkins whispered sharply.

"It's not your fault." Moreland said.

Wilkins shook his head again. "My command. My responsibility."

Once again Moreland realized how poor she was at comforting people. Before she could think of something else to say there was a scraping sound just around the corner of the tent. Moreland stared towards the front of the tent. A moment later a soldier staggered into the space between the two tents.

The soldier lifted the gun he was carrying and pointed it at Moreland. She still held her gun in hand, but something made her freeze.

"Corporal Dylan?" Moreland said. "It's me. Doctor Moreland."

Dylan's eyes were distant. It seemed like he wasn't in there. Still, he didn't fire the gun. He just stood there.

A gun shot banged suddenly. Thoughts raced through Moreland's head. She didn't feel any pain. She looked at the gun in her hand that pointed off in another direction, but did not seemed to have gone off. And then there was the left side of Dylan's head that appeared to explode.

Dylan fell to the ground and Wilkins stepped over the body. Moreland just then realized that Wilkins was not next to her. She understood he had gone back inside the tent and then out through the front and came up next to Corporal Dylan.

Wilkins shook his head. His voice was a little choked up. "I knew that kid."

"So did I." Moreland said softly.

"Come on. We have to go." Wilkins said and helped Moreland to her feet.

They had walked about half the distance back to the platform before either of them spoke.

"What about your men?" Moreland asked.

Wilkins was two steps ahead of her. He shook his head. "If they don't answer the radio, which is protocol, then they can't."

"What if they are just injured?" Moreland asked.

Wilkins glanced back at her. His look told her that he knew he might be leaving them there to die—-if they weren't dead already.

"The mission are these soil samples. A lot of other lives may depend on these." Wilkins said.

They stopped when they came to the ice wall. They had missed the platform. Wilkins and Moreland exchanged a look and then Wilkins waved to their right. They turned and walked along the ice wall. Moreland knew it was just a guess on which direction to go, but minutes later the shape of the platform materialized out of the fog.

They stepped on to the platform and buckled themselves in. Wilkins called up to the soldiers to lift them up. There was no answer. He tried two more times. Still nothing.

"If something has happened up there," Moreland said, "I don't think I can do another ice climb. You'll have to take the samples up yourself."

Wilkins looked at her. He shook his head and called on the radio again. This time they got an answer and within minutes the platform started climbing back up.

When the platform was too high for anyone below getting at them Moreland breathed a sigh of relief. She never wanted to go back to the Trench again.

The platform cleared the edge of the Trench and was lowered down on to the ice. They unbuckled themselves and walked off the platform.

A soldier came up to Wilkins.

"What the hell's going on up here?" Wilkins demanded.

"Sorry sir. We were trying to get a hold of someone at the Main camp." The soldier answered.

"Are they not answering?" Wilkins asked.

The soldier shook his head. "No sir."

"Shit." Moreland said standing just behind Wilkins.

"Keep trying." Wilkins said and the soldier turned and headed back to the radio equipment. Wilkins turned and looked at Moreland.

"Already been down this path." Moreland said. "It doesn't end well."

Wilkins didn't say anything. He just looked at Moreland.

Part 3 – The Ticking Clock

1

"We're trapped in here." Jessica said.

"Or...we're safe in here. Depends on your perspective." Mason said.

"Yeah, but even if they get back with the soil samples and you figure out a cure for this thing, how do we call your headquarters to tell them not to blow us up?" Jessica asked.

"The Army already knows what's going on here. Including the fact that I am working on something to combat the virus. Whatever help they are sending us is likely already enroute." Mason said.

Jessica nodded. "OK. Well, that sounds good." She sat on a stool in the lab for a minute thinking.

"Wait." Jessica said. "What if their *help* is to nuke us?"

Mason stopped measuring out a liquid into a beaker and turned to look at Jessica. "In that event then our help will be arriving sooner rather than later."

Jessica visibly did not like that answer. She was about to say something when there were gun shots. These were were loud. Too loud to be outside the building. Jessica and Mason looked at one another.

"They got inside." Jessica said. Her voice trembled. "Devon. Where is Devon?"

Mason set down a beaker, rummaged through a drawer and pulled a gun out. He checked the to see that the gun was loaded and crossed the room. He locked the door to the lab and turned to Jessica.

"Get over there. Between those cabinets." Mason said.

Jessica hesitated. She wanted to know what happened to Devon, but more shots convinced her to squeeze between a couple of the cabinets. She peeked out at Mason standing in front of the locked door.

"You think a locked door with a big glass window is going to stop crazed killers that just broke through a barricaded door?" Jessica asked.

Mason looked back at Jessica. "It's a lab, not a bunker. It's all we've got."

Mason crossed the room and squeezed down in front of Jessica. He was down on one knee watching the door.

Minutes passed and then they heard someone trying to open the door.

"Who is it?" Jessica whispered in Mason's ear.

Mason shook his head. "Can't tell. There's glare across the glass."

Mason felt Jessica's hand on his shoulder. She was squeezing hard.

"Jessica?" A voice came through the door.

"Shit. That's Devon." Jessica said. She tried climbing over Mason to get out.

"Control yourself, girl." Mason said falling to one side as Jessica moved past him.

Jessica scrambled across the room and unlocked the door and hugged Devon as he stepped into the room.

"What's going on?" Mason asked as he stood up and approached Devon.

"Wells." Devon said. "He...turned on us. Starting firing wildly down the hall."

"Wells?" Mason asked.

"Yes sir." Devon answered. "We had to kill him."

Jessica hugged Devon again. "I'm just glad you're alright."

"I'm fine." Devon said.

Jessica tensed up. She turned to look at Mason. "Jason turned...into one of them. Does that mean..."

Mason shook his head. "I don't know what that means. Everyone reacts differently to the virus and to the immune system booster I gave you."

"But it could happen to me too." Jessica said. Tears started down her face. Devon put an arm around her.

"I'm sure the others will be back soon." Devon said.

"Wells lasted quite a while from the booster shot." Mason said.

Jessica still looked worried. "That doesn't really make me feel much better."

Mason shrugged. "I will remind you that I am an Army doctor. A good bedside manner is not a job requirement."

"No shit." Jessica said.

The power flickered and then a minute later came back on.

"Nice work." Mason said. He clearly looked relieved. He knew without power they weren't going to be able to create some kind of vaccine, but he had chosen not to burden anyone else with that information. He was just trusting that Taylor knew they had the get the generators back on line.

"We're back in business." Mason said.

Jessica nodded and then a thought occurred to her and she quickly looked at Mason. "Wait, were you not going to be able to do the curing thing with the power off?"

Mason glanced briefly at Jessica. "Let's just say that it would have been difficult."

"You didn't say anything about that." Jessica said.

"Would it have made you feel any better if I had?" Mason asked.

Jessica hesitated. "Uh, no...but..."

"Well, there you go." Mason said.

2

The LMTVs sat idling. Wilkins, Moreland and two soldiers stood out in front of the vehicles with binoculars staring into the distance.

"That doesn't look good." Moreland said.

Wilkins sighed. "No. It doesn't."

Wilkins reached over to his walkie-talkie. "Anyone in Main camp. This is Major Wilkins."

He waited as he had the first few attempts to contact the camp. No answer.

"Damn it. Why doesn't anyone answer?" Wilkins said.

"Does everyone carry those?" Moreland asked. She pointed at the walkie-talkie.

Wilkins sighed. "No. Not unless they are in a combat situation."

"And this isn't one of those situations?" Moreland asked.

Wilkins glanced over at Moreland. "This was not a *planned* combat situation."

"Right." Moreland said.

"There." One of the soldiers said pointing. "That's the building the lab is in."

Wilkins and Moreland checked where the soldier was pointing and then looked again through their binoculars. It took a moment for them to focus in on it.

"Well, it still looks intact." Wilkins said.

"But we don't know what might be going on inside." Moreland said.

"You tend to see the negative side of things." Wilkins commented.

Moreland lowered her binoculars and looked at him. "I have stood over the bloody murdered body of my mentor, been exposed to a deadly virus, almost killed by numerous zombie soldiers, was almost blown up, ice climbed a fucking monster ice wall and nearly froze to death. I am kind short on optimism for this place."

Wilkins lowered his binoculars and looked at Moreland. He nodded slightly. "Point taken."

Wilkins waved the two soldiers closer. "We have to assume there are hostiles present in the camp. If we just drive right in we will likely draw any and all hostiles to us. Not knowing their numbers I don't like that strategy."

The two soldiers standing with Wilkins nodded in agreement.

"So, I want to roll in as close as we can without drawing any more attention than we have to. Then we'll try to work our way to the lab avoiding confrontation as much as possible. Got it?" Wilkins said.

The soldiers nodded. They turned to pass the plan on to the rest of the men.

Wilkins turned to Moreland. "You heard that?"

Moreland nodded.

Wilkins nodded in return. "OK. Once we disembark from the LMTVs you will carry the samples and stay in the middle of the group. OK?"

"OK." Moreland said.

"Good. Let's get this done." Wilkins said and the two of them headed back to the vehicles.

They drew to within a short distance of the camp and stopped. The group formed up and began approaching the northeast corner of the Main camp. While the camp looked to be in some disarray they didn't see anybody moving about.

They reached the corner of the nearest Quonset hut. Wilkins adjusted their order slightly and quietly went over the route they would try to take. They all understood their biggest issue at the moment was that the building holding the infirmary and the lab was located almost in the center of the camp. It meant that at some point they were going to be exposed on all sides.

Slowly they crept forward. It took what felt like an interminably long time to Moreland just to reach the front of the Quonset hut. They scanned the area and still saw nothing. Ahead of them was a double row of mobile trailers. Past that were several buildings, one of which was the infirmary.

Two soldiers crossed the open space to reach the first trailer. They gave a thumbs up back to Wilkins. Two more soldiers were ready to cross the open space, but didn't go. A sound drew their attention. Wilkins stood next to them and saw it too.

An infected soldier appeared from around the far front corner of the Quonset hut. He was armed. He moved slowly towards them. Wilkins turned to a soldier behind him he made some quick hand gestures and the soldier turned and ran back in the direction they had come from.

Wilkins and the two soldiers in the front pulled back behind the corner to stay out of the infected soldier's line of fire. Wilkins peered carefully around the corner. The infected soldier continued to move towards them and was clearly trying to lift his gun to shoot.

Moments later another soldier turned the corner behind the infected soldier. It took only a moment for the soldier from their group to dispatch the infected soldier. He drove a knife quietly through the back of the infected soldier and dropped his body where it had stood. He nodded to Wilkins.

Wilkins nodded in return. He turned and patted the two soldiers next to him and sent them across the open space. They joined their two comrades waiting next to the trailer. Minutes later all of them had cleared the open space.

They regrouped next to the trailer and then began moving past the first set of trailers. The space between the trailer they were next to and the next row of trailers was cluttered with stacked pallets and crates. As they were easing past the pallets there was the sudden sound of movement and the clicking of automatic rifles coming off safety.

Multiple soldiers in their group spun to their left, guns ready. They were greeted by several soldiers with guns pointed at them in return. Both groups hesitated and seemed to be waiting for something.

"Wait." Wilkins said. "Stand down."

The soldiers in Wilkins group seemed unsure, but slightly lowered their guns.

"Major Wilkins?" A whispered voice came from the other group.

"Taylor?" Wilkins asked.

Sergeant Taylor lowered his weapon and pushed past a couple of the guys with him. "Damned glad to see you sir."

"You too." Wilkins said. "How many of you are there?"

"Five, sir." Taylor replied.

"Any idea how many hostiles?" Wilkins asked.

Taylor shook his head slightly. "Hard to say sir. Some of them appear to be dead until you get near them and then, well, they're like a booby trap."

Wilkins nodded. "Understood. OK. We have to get these samples to the lab."

"Yes sir." Taylor said. "We just got one of the generators back up. To restore power back to the lab."

"Is everyone in the lab OK?" Moreland asked.

Taylor hesitated. "As far as I know, ma'am. I haven't communicated with them for a little while though."

"Hey," Wilkins said to Taylor, "is no one carrying a walkie-talkie?"

Taylor shrugged. "We were kind of taken by surprise by all this. There are some in the weapons locker, but its way the hell over at the other end."

"Wonderful. OK. We need to go. Time is not our friend." Wilkins said.

Taylor nodded. "The building is just beyond that one." Taylor turned and pointed.

Wilkins nodded. "That's what I was thinking."

"It's kind of open over there. More open than what you just came across." Taylor said.

"Yeah. I remember." Wilkins said. "No choice."

"Right." Taylor said. "we'll take point and secure the area in front of the door. We'll lay down any cover if you need it."

"Good. Lead on." Wilkins said.

Taylor nodded and he and his men moved down through the pallets and crates to the other end of the trailer. The rest followed them. At the corner they scanned for any infected soldiers. Seeing no one they moved to the front corner of the trailer. Taking just a moment they gestured their readiness and made sure everyone was in agreement.

At a sprint Taylor and his men crossed the space between the trailer and the back side of the infirmary. At the back of the building Taylor moved to a door while his men deployed in a small perimeter around him. Taylor pounded on the door.

"Sergeant Taylor. We have welcome guests." Taylor called through the door. It took a minute for the door to open up. Taylor had a short conversation with the person inside the doorway and then stepped back from the door. He turned and waved to Wilkins.

Wilkins gave quick instructions to his men and then, as a group, they all started across the open area.

The moment they were out in the open Moreland realized that Wilkins had organized his men in a rough circle around her. They were a living, moving shield. She wasn't sure if it was to protect her or the samples. She was, at least, hoping it was a little of both.

They were about a third of the way across when what had been a dead body lying on the ground a short distance away lifted up. The infected soldier looked to be in pretty rough shape. He lifted a rifle and tried to take aim at them.

One of Taylor's men spotted him and fired off a couple of rounds. The body dropped back down and didn't move.

As they closed on the open door bullets shots seemed to suddenly start banging all around them. Wilkins turned and saw a nearby body holding an M18 and firing. The soldier's head was face planted into the ground, but his hand was just randomly firing off shots.

Wilkins twisted to his left and fired two rounds into the back of the soldier's head. The hand holding the M18 dropped it.

Moments later all of them ducked through the open door and with a resounding bang the door slammed shut.

3

Jessica leaned her head on to Devon's chest. "I'm afraid."

Devon put an arm around her. "I think we're still safe in here."

"No." Jessica said. "I mean I'm afraid I will turn into one of those crazy killers and...you'll have to kill me."

Devon took her by the shoulders and leaned her back a little. He looked at her. "No one is going to kill you. We'll figure this all out."

Jessica sighed. "I'm feeling...you know, tired again."

Devon glanced over at Mason who was leaning against a counter that ran along one wall.

Mason shrugged. "I don't know. I've given her another, smaller, dose of the booster, but there's only so much of that I can give her. At some point her immune system will have to either beat this thing or..."

"Or I go crazy?" Jessica said turning to look at Mason.

Mason didn't really want to answer that and he didn't have to. There was a loud banging on the door down the hallway.

The three of them exchanged a quick look.

"Maybe that's Sergeant Taylor. Maybe he's cleared all the infected soldiers from the camp." Devon said.

"All but one." Jessica said.

Devon rubbed Jessica's shoulder. He turned and ducked down the hall. Jessica was going to follow him, but Mason pulled her back into the room.

"We don't know what that is yet." Mason said.

Devon joined Eddie at the door. Eddie's left arm was bandaged from where Wells had tried to kill him.

The banging repeated and before they could form a plan a voice called to them from outside.

"Sergeant Taylor." Eddie said and began clearing the door to open it. Devon hesitated. He wondered if the zombie soldiers were smart enough to pretend to be someone else.

"Help me." Eddie said over his shoulder.

Devon decided he didn't really think zombies could mimic someone's voice. He stepped forward and helped Eddie finish clearing the door. Eddie opened the door slightly and peeked out. A moment later he opened the door wide.

"Glad to see you Sarge." Eddie said.

Taylor nodded at Eddie. "We've got some people that need to get in here. Stand by." Taylor turned and signaled Wilkins.

A minute passed and Eddie could see people crossing the open space between their building and the line of trailers. He heard shots and someone just outside the door returned fire. The people kept coming. When they were almost to the door when more shots rang out.

Devon stepped forward to try to see what was happening. More shots were fired and then a burst of people came through the door. Eddie and Devon had to jump back to allow everyone to pile into the hallway. The last soldier through the door slammed it shut.

"Scotty." Moreland said and gave Devon a hug. "How's Jessica?"

Devon shrugged. "OK, I guess. She's still fighting the virus."

"Good. Well, we have what Major Mason wanted." Moreland slid a container out of one of her pockets and held it up.

"Then I guess we should get it to the lab." Devon said. They turned and headed down the hall. Behind them Wilkins was getting a briefing from both Taylor and Eddie on what had been going on in the Main camp.

When Moreland walked into the lab Jessica ran over to her and hugged her. Moreland felt like the hugging might be getting a little out of control. It's true she had hugged Devon when she saw him, but she knew that part of her reaction was due to the fact that she was so happy that she had made it back alive.

Moreland passed the containers over to Mason who immediately started prepping them.

"You made it." Jessica said happily.

"At faster than smashed turtle speed too." Moreland said.

Jessica nodded. "Yeah. A little better than that I guess."

"Hey," Moreland said holding up her M18, "I got one."

"Wow. Look at you, a zombie killing bitch." Jessica said.

Down the hall they could here activity as the soldiers barricaded up the door again and sorted out their security plans. Minutes later Wilkins and Taylor stood in the doorway of the lab.

"Dr. Moreland, your assistance please." Mason said over his shoulder.

Moreland walked over to the counter where Mason was working.

"You know I'm a paleontologist, right?" Moreland asked.

Mason glanced over at her. "You have a PhD and two hands, right?"

"Yeah." Moreland said with a shrug. "Still, I'm far more accustomed with working on dead things that aren't still moving."

Mason stopped and looked at Moreland. "Uh...you understand that these men are not dead, right? These men are very much alive."

The room was silent for a moment.

"What?" Taylor said. "You mean we've been killing our own?"

"Son of a bitch." Wilkins said. He looked at Mason. "These men could be cured?"

Mason nodded. "If I can find a way to neutralize the virus, yes."

"Damn it!" Wilkins took a step into the room. He stared at Mason. "That would have been good to know. Like days ago. You know, before I was killing my own men."

Mason stared back at Wilkins. "And what, Major, would you have done? Asked the infected soldiers to put down their weapons or face disciplinary action?"

"Fuck you." Wilkins said. "We would have tried to do something other than gun them down." Wilkins stormed out of the room.

Mason looked around the room. Everyone was looking at him. Taylor, in particular, was staring hard at Mason.

"What the hell did you think these soldiers were?" Mason asked.

For a moment no one said anything.

"Uh, zombies." Jessica said.

Mason's mouth dropped open. "What idiot thinks that zombies are anything more than horror film props?"

Again, no one spoke.

"Unfucking believable." Mason said. He turned and capped off a beaker. He turned back to Taylor.

"Sergeant, we are going to need communications restored with McMurdo. That, and the security of this building are the two top priorities." Mason said.

Taylor hesitated for just a second. "Yes sir." His tone was sharp.

"And one more thing. Private Wells' body is in a room down the hall. That needs to removed from the building. The bodies of the infected dead are even more dangerous than the living ones."

Taylor clearly wanted say something. Instead he just gave a curt nod and left the room.

"Zombies." Jessica whispered to Moreland.

Mason turned and glanced over at Jessica. "Not zombies. It just so happens that the dead bodies are more contagious than the living infected people are."

"Is that normal?" Moreland asked.

Mason shook his head. "No. That's not normal. For a virus. Typically a virus thrives in a living host. A dead host, though, would at least mean its immune system would begin to fail. Bacteria certainly likes it that way. So, I suppose, there is a certain evolutionary advantage to this particular virus. Still, not generally what we see."

Moreland thought for a moment. "Do you think this virus prefers a dead host?"

Mason looked at Moreland. "Prefers? It's not like it can pick and choose the state of it's targets."

"It could if it could change the host's behavior." Moreland said.

Mason looked at Moreland skeptically. "We discussed that already. There's no precedent for that. I can't buy into that theory. It strikes me as a bit too much like science fiction. These soldiers are trained to kill people. The virus causes a fever that spikes high and the soldiers are just resorting to the training that is embedded in their brain. That's all."

Moreland shook her head. "The layout of the fossils at the dig site clearly indicate that the Morrosaurus were killing each other. Based on the small percentage of the fossils we had uncovered and the sheer number of fossils found by the USR it's got to be statistically impossible for us to dig up the only animals attacking each other. The only logical conclusion is that the majority of the Morrosaurus were killing each other."

Mason sighed. "Did you consider the possibility that your initial premise is wrong?"

"My initial premise?" Moreland asked.

"That these Morro..." Mason started.

"Morbidsaurus." Jessica volunteered.

Moreland looked at Jessica. "What the hell."

"Whatever." Mason said waving a hand in the air. "The premise that these creatures have behavioral characteristics you are unaware of."

Moreland shook her head. "No. We have massive fossil record many of which depict whole animal scenes and none of the herbivore species demonstrate this kind of behavior. Nor do any living descendants of the dinosaurs exhibit what we saw at the dig site."

Mason shook his head skeptically.

"And..." Moreland started.

"And?" Mason asked.

"Something Beecham said." Moreland thought for a moment. "He said it felt like someone else was in the driver's seat. Those were his exact words."

Mason just looked at Moreland for a moment. He shook his head slightly. "I don't know. Doesn't seem realistic to me, but, Doctor, if your theory turns out to be true then it's all the more reason we need to stop this damned thing."

4

Mason looked at his watch. "We have about twenty more minutes. Then we can pull those out. If I've got the ratio right we should see a nearly clean slide."

"You mean no live virus?" Moreland asked.

"Yes. Exactly." Mason said. "When we pull it I need you to transfer a sample on to the slide. I will get the other two prepped."

"Understood." Moreland said with a nod.

Jessica sat quietly in the corner. The look in her eyes was one of someone on the verge of exhaustion.

Wilkins had come into the room a short while earlier. He stood leaning against the wall by the door. He too had been quiet. In his case it was a brooding quiet.

"I don't mean to question your capabilities, Major Mason, but how exactly does an Army doctor in a place like this have the know how to find a cure for a never before seen some prehistoric virus?" Wilkins asked.

Mason had been leaning over and staring into the incubator at the small clear plastic containers holding several samples. He stood up, but did not turn to look at Wilkins. For a moment it seemed like he was going to ignore Wilkins' question.

"Because," Mason said, "before this I was stationed in Maryland."

"Maryland? Why is the Army in Maryland? Who would invade that state?" Jessica asked.

Everyone looked at Jessica. She put her hands up questioningly.

Moreland didn't understand the reference either, but because Jessica asked the question she assumed it was a stupid question and decided not to say anything.

Wilkins studied Mason for a minute. A thought came to him. "Oh. Bio weapons. You worked on bio weapon research." Wilkins "So why are you here?"

Mason looked at Wilkins. "I got tired of the work I was doing. High pressure. It is the kind of work you spend your whole life doing and hope that everything you've done is a waste of time. That wears on you after a while. Why am I here? A good place to tuck someone away, isn't it?" Mason said with a slight shrug.

Wilkins nodded, but didn't say anything.

"I don't want to be a zombie." Jessica said quietly. She was staring down at her boots.

Mason had leaned back over to glance into the incubator again. "Not a zombie."

"So," Moreland said, "if you just restrained an infected person so they couldn't hurt anyone else or themselves, couldn't their own immune system eventually fight the virus off?"

Mason straightened up again. He looked at Moreland and shook his head. "Tried that. Eventually the virus drives the fever so high it begins to destroy the brain."

Jessica begin sobbing a little.

Mason turned to look at Jessica. He walked over to where she sat and knelt down in front of her. "Look, this virus is not that unique. It has numerous similarities to some common current viruses. In addition, it seems similar to some viruses I have worked with at DARPA. The booster I gave you contains much of the base we will use to break this virus down and destroy it. I think what's cooking in the incubator now will destroy the virus. It has enzymes that will disrupt the cells of the virus from manipulating proteins."

Jessica looked confused. "I think that sounded good."

"It was good." Moreland said.

Jessica looked at Mason. "Look at you, all full of comforty shit."

Mason shrugged and returned to the incubator on the counter.

Moreland moved over next to Mason.

"How long do you think it will take to come up with something if the results from this are what you hope they are?" Moreland quietly asked.

Mason gave her a quick glance. He knew she was worried about Jessica. "A couple of hours."

Moreland peered back over her shoulder at Jessica. "If you had to guess...how long has she got?"

Mason shook his head slightly. "I honestly don't know. This thing is so dependent on the strength of each individual's immune system there is almost no way to gauge it. The body will fight it right up until the breaking point. After that, well, it's like a dike giving way. The collapse happens relatively fast."

Moreland sighed and nodded.

When Mason determined the time in the incubator was complete the two of them began preparing slides. It was slow and careful work.

Devon came into the lab. He went over to Jessica and talked to her quietly for a few minutes. He stood up and turned to looked Mason and Moreland. They were bent over the counter working and had their backs to him.

"I'm going to find something for Jessica to eat. Do either of you need anything?" Devon asked.

Mason didn't even look back at Devon. He just waved a dismissive hand back at him. Moreland turned around. She smiled at Devon.

"No. Scotty, but thank you." Moreland said.

Devon nodded. He gave Jessica a quick smile and left the room.

Jessica seemed to be dozing off in the chair. She didn't wake up at the sound of some gun fire outside of the building.

Minutes passed and Taylor entered the lab. Wilkins stood just behind him in the hallway.

"Sir." Taylor stood in the doorway looking at Mason's back.

Mason turned. "What's our status?"

Taylor sighed. "Well, quite a bit of the communication equipment was damaged, but we have cobbled together as much as we can."

"And?" Mason asked.

"And...there are a couple of pieces we still need. What we had here was damaged beyond repair. With our supply building partially destroyed we do not have spares available." Taylor said.

Wilkins slid past Taylor and into the room. "Sergeant Taylor has told me what they need and I think we might have those parts at the Upper camp. Last time we were there the supply tent was still intact."

"Well, we will need to get the communications up. After the work we are doing here communications are the next priority. Before headquarters does anything rash." Mason said.

Wilkins nodded. "We could retrieve what we need from the Upper camp."

Mason shook his head. "That would take hours to get out there and back."

"If we drove out, yes, but if we flew we could do it in about an hour." Wilkins said.

"Flew? I thought all the choppers were burned?" Mason asked.

"We did too, but we found the Little Bird parked out beyond the vehicles." Taylor said.

"Little Bird?" Moreland said.

Wilkins glanced over at her. "It's an AH-6 helicopter. Two seats. Well, you can sit a few guys on external benches."

"Who has to sit out there?" Moreland asked.

Wilkins smiled at her. "Whoever is ordered to."

"Oh." Moreland said with a nod.

Wilkins looked at Mason. "Sergeant Taylor and I could ride out there and get what we need."

Mason thought about if for a moment. "Take two soldiers with you. We should be able to afford that."

Wilkins nodded. He glanced over at Taylor and the two of them headed back out the door of the lab.

Moreland looked at Mason. "What did you mean by your headquarters doing something rash?"

"He means nuking us." Jessica said from where she was sitting.

Moreland turned to look at Jessica. She didn't realize Jessica had woke up. Then she looked at Mason.

"What? Nuking us?" Moreland asked.

Mason looked at Moreland. "That would be one of the contingency plans."

"Well, that's a shitty plan." Moreland said.

Mason's expression indicated he was puzzled. "I thought you were prepared to shoot yourself back at the Upper camp to stop the virus from spreading."

Moreland hesitated. She glanced over at Jessica who shrugged back at her. "Yeah...well, that was different."

"How so?" Mason asked.

"Because...I was choosing my own fate." Moreland said.

"But...the net result would be the same." Mason pointed out.

"Yeah...well, I don't think I like their *contingency plan* at all." Moreland said.

"Yeah, well, there ain't no warm and fuzzies in the Army." Jessica said.

Mason pointed at Jessica. "She gets it."

"Oh, I get it." Moreland said. "I just think it sucks."

5

"You're sure you know how to fly this thing?" Wilkins asked. He looked over at Taylor.

"I got it. I got it." Taylor said correcting the helicopter as it slid hard to their left. "God damned cross wind."

"How long has it been since you flew one of these?" Wilkins asked.

Taylor glanced quickly at Wilkins. "A while."

"Don't let it worry you that all our lives might depend on our successfully getting the communications up and running." Wilkins said.

"Sounds like some sarcasm there Major. I think you've hanging out too much with that scientist woman." Taylor said.

Wilkins sighed. "Maybe so."

Outside the Little Bird on each side sat a soldier on the exterior benches. Wilkins did not envy them. It had to be cold as hell out there.

It took them about thirty minutes to cover the distance back to the Upper camp. Wilkins saw the camp slowly growing larger as they drew near. It sure beat crawling at about ten miles per hour over the fractured ice.

"Not too close." Wilkins said to Taylor.

Taylor nodded and pointed to a spot about a hundred yards out from the nearest tent. Wilkins gave him a thumbs up and Taylor zeroed the Little Bird in on to the spot. The landing was a bit of a jolt, but they were down and in one piece.

As all four of them disembarked from the helicopter Wilkins gestured for them to crouch down. Taylor and Wilkins both scanned the camp with binoculars. There was no visible activity.

"Nothing." Taylor said.

"Right now." Wilkins said. "The boys I lost in the Trench were ambushed by what appeared to be dead soldiers."

Taylor nodded. "We saw that too. It's like they can just lay there in the cold without moving until you get near them."

"Yeah." Wilkins stood up. "Let's go."

The others stood up as well. They spread out a little so they didn't become a single target and started walking towards the closest tents.

They walked in silence for a short distance.

"Permission to speak freely, sir?" Taylor asked.

Wilkins nodded. "Go ahead."

"Major Mason." Taylor said.

Wilkins took in a cold breath. He breathed it out slowly. "Yeah."

"He should have told us the guys weren't zombies." Taylor said.

Wilkins glanced sideways at Taylor. "Well, common sense should have told you they weren't zombies."

"Fuck. I know that, but he should have told us they weren't dead, I mean, that they could be saved." Taylor said.

"Yeah." Wilkins said. "He should have told us that."

"God damn it." Taylor said. "I...killed—-"

"I know, soldier." Wilkins said sharply. "I killed some of my own men too. I know. This issue is still open and I will pursue this matter further. That is, though, assuming we live through this."

"Right." Taylor said. "Wrestle the gator in front of you."

Wilkins looked over at Taylor. "Where are you from?"

"Florida, sir." Taylor answered.

Wilkins shook his head. "I'm not even going to ask what you boys down there do in your spare time."

"Shots of whiskey and gators, sir." Taylor said with a smile.

"I could use a shot right now, but you can keep the damned gator." Wilkins said.

They were quiet for a couple of minutes.

"Sir?" Taylor asked.

"Yeah." Wilkins said.

"How are we going to handle the guys now?" Taylor asked.

"What guys?" Wilkins asked.

"The infected ones." Taylor said. "I don't want to kill any more if they can be saved."

"Right." Wilkins said. "Not sure. They don't seemed to be very aware of what they're doing. We're going to have to find ways to knock them out, I guess."

"And not get killed in the process." Taylor said.

"Yeah." Wilkins said glancing over at Taylor. "That would kind of undermine the whole point of trying to save someone's life."

Taylor nodded. "Right. And you might want to not hang out with that snarky woman as much."

Wilkins smiled and shook his head.

They came up to the first tent. They still hadn't seen any movement. Nor did they hear anything. It seemed like a ghost town.

They circle the first few tents and still nothing moved in the camp. Wilkins glanced around the corner of the tent they were next to. He turned and indicated to Taylor and the other soldiers that the larger tent just beyond was their target. They nodded in agreement.

Slowly they moved to the front of the supply tent and eased quietly into it. An eerie silence still seemed to hang about them.

"Alright. Let's spread out and look for the boxes that are labeled as communication equipment. I wish I could tell you where to start, but I didn't organize this place." Wilkins said.

"Right." Taylor said. He turned, looked at the other two soldiers, and pointed in a couple of directions. "You guys start over there."

All four of them spent most of an hour digging into pallets of boxes and crawling on top of stacked pallets looking for the appropriate markings.

"Here." One of the soldiers called out. The other three converged on him. The soldier pointed to a box that someone had written in marker down side 'Comm parts'.

All three stared at the box and its location for a moment. It was buried in the middle of a pallet that had two more pallets of boxes and crates stacked on top of it.

"Well..." Wilkins said.

"Yeah." Taylor said. "We're not moving those top pallets unless we unload them."

Wilkins shook his head. "As tight as it is here between the surrounding pallets if we just throw everything off the top pallets we're going to bury the bottom one. We would have to carry all that stuff somewhere else and toss it out of the way. That could take us another hour or more."

"We need a forklift." One of the soldiers suggested.

Wilkins shook his head again. "We would have to scout around the camp for a forklift. Hope the damned thing is in working order. Get it here. Then move those first two stacks out of the way just so we could get at this stack."

"And not get killed while looking or driving the forklift here." Taylor added.

Wilkins nodded. "And not get ambushed. Right."

They stood for a minute quietly staring at the pallets again.

"Fuck it." Taylor said. He waved the rest of them back. When all of them were further away from their target stack he swung his XM7 up and started firing at the middle pallet.

At first Wilkins thought Taylor had just gotten pissed off, but as he watched he realized what Taylor was doing. Taylor was shooting at the boxes on the bottom of the middle pallet on the side opposite of where the box they were after.

It was hard to tell if the other two soldiers understood what Taylor was doing or if they just thought it seemed like fun, but they joined in. Cardboard, wood, small pieces of metal and plastic were flying in all directions.

After just a couple of minutes it became obvious Taylor's idea was going to work. Their shooting had chewed through a significant amount of material on the middle pallet and it was now, slowly, starting to tilt forward. Another thirty seconds and the middle pallet and the top pallet leaned precariously and then in an instant they crashed forward on top of the two pallets next to them.

The net result was that the backside of the bottom pallet, in the general area the box they were after was located was partially exposed. From there they could cut their way down into the box and fish out what they needed.

They had stopped shooting when the pallets fell over. Taylor looked at Wilkins.

"Improvise and adapt." Taylor said with a smile.

"Damn straight." Wilkins smiled back. "Let's get to it."

The two soldiers and Taylor climbed over the mess and back down in between pallets on the far side. They pulled out knives and began hacking their way through the boxes.

Wilkins stood next the pile of debris. All four of them could not fit back there. He waited for them to find what they were after. A couple of minutes passed before one of them called out. He held up one of the components they were looking for. They passed it out to Wilkins.

Wilkins studied the box for a moment confirming that it was indeed what they needed. Taylor and the other soldiers were now digging deep into the pallet. They were all focused on their search when the shots rang out.

"Shit." Wilkins said.

Taylor saw Wilkins drop to the ground. He knew from the sound of Wilkins' voice he had been hit. He wanted to climb back over the pallet and see how badly Wilkins was hit, but rounds kept tearing into pallets all around them. They were pinned down with no way to help Wilkins—-if he was even still alive.

6

Mason stood up. He nodded as he looked back down at the microscope. He slapped the counter. "Yeah. That's it."

Both Moreland and Jessica jumped at the sound.

"Dead?" Moreland asked.

Mason looked over at her and nodded again. "Yeah. Dead."

"That's great. So, you can build a vaccine from that?" Moreland asked.

"Yeah. It's just folding this into the base I already have." Mason said. "I suspected the original form contained the inherent flaw that could be exploited. Just needed to be sure it was there. Otherwise the vaccine would only affect the few mutated strains I've already seen."

"So, we're just lucky that this virus has a vulnerability?" Moreland asked.

Mason shook his head as he began shifting equipment around. "No. All species have vulnerabilities. For every strong characteristic in any given species there are weaknesses. It's like Nature only provides a set amount of strengths. If certain characteristics become enhanced others become weaker."

"You mean like in people?" Jessica asked. "You've got smart people and stupid people."

"Not exactly." Mason said. "These are physiological traits."

"So, you had already spotted a vulnerability in this virus and just needed to know that the original form had the vulnerability so that all subsequent mutations likely would carry the same vulnerability that you could target." Moreland said.

"Exactly. There is a protein that when the virus is exposed to it causes it to lose cellular cohesion." Mason explained.

"Cellular cohesion?" Jessica looked at Mason.

"It melts like butter." Moreland said.

"Yes." Mason said.

"Well, then butter me up, Doc." Jessica said.

Moreland shook her head. "Not an appropriate way to refer to that."

"And I guessed earlier that I might be able to utilize something like that. So, I already built a base the I need only alter slightly to do the trick." Mason said.

Jessica waved at Mason. "OK. Get to it and let's turn this trick."

"Again, what's wrong with you? That is totally not the way to describe this." Moreland said.

Jessica smiled. "Did I tell you that I'm having Scotty's baby?"

"What?" Moreland stared at Jessica. Her mind started spinning. When had Jessica and Scotty even had time for sex in all this? And how could Jessica even know she was pregnant at this point?

"What are you talking about?" Moreland asked.

"And we are going to live in Pittsburgh." Jessica said confidently.

"Pittsburgh? Why would you want to live in Pittsburgh?" Moreland was confused.

"Wait, have I ever been to Pittsburgh?" Jessica asked.

"How would I know?" Moreland said. "Are you alright? What's going on?"

"Am I a zombie now?" Jessica asked looking at Mason. "Funny, I don't feel like eating anyone's brains."

"What the hell?" Moreland turned to look at Mason.

Mason walked over to Jessica. He felt her forehead. He reached back and grabbed the thermometer and took her temperature.

"Her fever's spiking." Mason said setting the thermometer down.

"Shit. Shit." Moreland said. "What do we do?"

Mason hesitated.

"What?" Moreland asked.

"Sedate her and put her in an ice bath." Mason said.

"Won't that put her into shock?" Moreland asked.

"Maybe, but the fever surely will kill her." Mason replied. "We need to get her fever down quickly or...well, it won't be good."

"How quickly?" Moreland asked.

"Very quickly." Mason answered.

"So how do we do this?" Moreland asked.

"Distract her." Mason said.

"Where is Pittsburgh?" Jessica asked.

"How...oh fuck it." Moreland leaned forward and hugged Jessica. "I am so happy for you and Devon."

Devon walked into the lab and looked at Moreland hugging Jessica and Mason moving quickly across the room with a syringe in hand.

"Hi, honey. I'm home." Jessica said looking up at Devon.

Devon froze. "What the hell...?"

"Ow! Hey!" Jessica said.

Moreland looked at Devon. "She needs to be sedated. Her fever's up."

"She needs to go into an ice bath." Mason said.

"An ice bath? She could freeze to death in one of those things. Can't you—-" Devon said.

"Soldier." Mason said sharply. "That's an order. Get her to the immersion tank. It's two rooms down on the right. She'll die if you don't."

Devon straightened up. "Yes sir."

"You two get her down there and get the tank filled with cold water and any ice you can find." Mason said. "I need to finish the vaccine."

Jessica started slumping over. Moreland, with Devon's help, lifted her up from either side.

"Where is the ice kept?" Moreland asked.

"Usually we just bring some over from the mess hall, but obviously that's out of the question." Mason said. "There are some freezers in the building though. They're used for storing some medicines and a few of my medical experiments. Just chip some ice out of the sides of the freezers and toss that in."

"What the hell? This building is sitting on an ice sheet and we have to chip ice out of freezer to chill some water?" Moreland said.

"Oh, and by the way, when you go into the freezers, if you see any containers with red tape around them...well, don't touch them. And, for God's sake, don't knock out on to the floor." Mason said.

Moreland and Devon stopped in the doorway and turned slightly.

"Why? What's in them?" Moreland asked.

"You'll sleep better not knowing." Mason shrugged at them. "It gets a little boring around here—-well, I mean, it used to. Anyway, I have hobbies."

Moreland sighed. "Jesus, the fun around here just never stops."

"I think that was sarcasm..." Jessica's voice was slurred heavily.

It took them about a half hour to get Jessica, gallons of cold water and an odd assortment of ice chunks all into the immersion tank. It also took Devon holding Jessica by the shoulders to keep her in the cold water. When Jessica calmed down some Moreland headed back down the hall to help Mason with the vaccine.

Moreland walked into the lab to find Mason standing and staring at a short row of test tubes.

"Does staring at them do something?" Moreland asked.

Mason turned and looked at Moreland. "You're really good at that sarcasm shit."

Moreland nodded. "Lots of practice."

"Right. Well, I believe this is it." Mason waved a hand towards the test tubes.

"That's great. Can we get it into Jessica?" Moreland asked.

Mason hesitated.

"What?" Moreland asked.

Mason sighed. "As I said, I *believe* this is it."

"You're not sure?" Moreland looked at Mason with concern.

"Does this look like DARPA to you?" Mason asked.

"How would I know what the DARPA lab place looks like?" Moreland asked.

"I mean that working in a facility like this under these conditions, this is the best I could do. So, am I 100% sure this is it? No, but I think I'm close. However, I would prefer the first test subject was not Miss Jessica." Mason said.

"Oh. Right. Maybe not." Moreland said.

"Let's go check on our patient." Mason said.

The two of them went down the hall and into the room where the immersion tank was. Devon was still sitting next to the tank.

"Pull her out." Mason said.

Moreland and Devon lifted Jessica out. They laid in out on gurney that had been sitting against the wall. Mason check Jessica's temperature.

"OK. Let's get her back to a bed in the infirmary. Then we need to find our guinea pig." Mason said.

"Guinea Pig?" Devon asked.

"We need to find someone to test the vaccine on." Moreland said. Before Devon could say something Moreland continued. "The first test is a bit risky."

Devon hesitated and then nodded. After another moment a thought came to him. "But...aren't all of the other infected people outside?"

"Yup." Mason said. "We're going to need one of them."

"I'll bring one in." Devon said quickly.

Moreland shook her head. "I don't know about that. Jessica might need you in here."

"Jessica needs this vaccine." Devon said. It was obvious from his tone of voice that Devon was not going to change his mind on this.

"OK. Let's get it done. Get two volunteers. We need the subject to be in one piece. No major injuries. Understood?" Mason said.

"Yes sir." Devon replied.

"And be careful. We can't afford to lose anyone else at this point. You go get your volunteers and I will help get Miss Jessica back to the infirmary." Mason said.

"Yes sir." Devon nodded and left the room.

"How long will she hold out after this?" Moreland asked as she and Mason half carried and half dragged Jessica down the hall.

"Not sure." Mason said. "I tried this on a soldier early on. It kept the fever at bay for only a short time, but you can't keep dropping her into the ice water. At some point she will go into shock and we'll lose her."

"So now we just wait." Moreland said as they deposited Jessica into a bed.

"We wait." Mason acknowledged. "And hope that nothing extreme happens in the mean time."

Moreland glanced at Mason. "Like we get nuked?"

"Like we get nuked." Mason nodded slowly.

7

"Fuck this." Taylor said. He slid past one of the other soldiers and moved up to the corner of a pallet next to the great pile from their collapsed pallets. He took a quick peek around the corner and then lunged out landing on his side. He immediately started firing into a stack of pallets next to the infected soldier that had staggered into the supply tent opening fire at them.

Debris from the pallets next to the infected soldier rained down on him. The infected soldier's aim was, at best, haphazard. It was unfocused and only randomly hitting things. Whatever round that had struck Wilkins was blind luck.

After another few moments containers of some sort started falling out of an upper pallet and landing on the infected soldier. When the infected soldier's gun ceased firing Taylor waved another soldier out from behind their pallet and they jumped their attacker. A couple of quick strikes with the butt of their rifles and the sick soldier was out.

Taylor turned and quickly moved over to Wilkins. "Sir?"

Wilkins was laying on his left side. He wasn't moving. At Taylor's question, though, he twisted around to look at him.

"It's alright. A clean shot right through." Wilkins lifted a bloody hand from the side of his right thigh.

Taylor turned to one of the soldiers. "Get me something bind this thing."

With a nod the soldier was off scrambling around some pallets.

Taylor waved at the other soldier. "Scout around. No more surprises."

The other soldier nodded and moved through the pallets and crates in the general direction of the front of the supply tent.

The first soldier slid back down off a pallet next to Taylor and Wilkins. He handed Taylor a blanket. Taylor took out his knife and put a lengthy slit down the blanket creating a strip of cloth. He wrapped it around Wilkins leg and tied it as tight as he could.

"Can you walk on it?" Taylor asked.

Wilkins shrugged. "One way to find out." With help he stood up, but it was immediately obvious that he couldn't put much weight on his right leg.

Taylor put an arm around Wilkins to help him move, but Wilkins pushed his arm aside. "Get the other component. Then we'll worry about getting out of here."

"Right." Taylor said. He turned to the other soldier and waved for him to follow. They climbed back up into the pile that comprised the remnants of the pallet they were searching through. It took them another fifteen minutes to find what they were looking for. They slid down from the pallet with their prize.

"Nothing sir." Said the soldier that had been out scouting the area.

Taylor nodded. "Good. Let's get the hell out of here."

They stashed the components into a backpack. Taylor shouldered the backpack and then helped Wilkins while the other two soldiers took up positions in front and back of them.

"What do we do with him?" Taylor asked Wilkins as they passed the infected soldier they had subdued.

Wilkins shook his head. "Can't do anything for him right now. Mason is the only one that can help these guys now."

They stepped out of the supply tent and scanned the area. Nothing moved, but by now they knew that didn't mean much.

They headed back in the direction of the tents along the camp perimeter. They had only gone a short distance when Wilkins stopped them.

"It's going to take us an hour to get back to the Little Bird like this." Wilkins said. "Give me a rifle and set me down next to one of those tents."

Taylor shook his head slightly as he looked Wilkins in the eye. "No sir."

"Soldier, that's an order." Wilkins said.

Again Taylor shook his head. "No sir. Look, sir, the way I figure it we have lost a lot of good soldiers here. We can't lose any more."

The other two soldiers stood staring at Wilkins and Taylor. The look in their eyes echoed Taylor's look.

Taylor took the backpack off. He handed it to the soldier up front. He waved at that soldier to grab Wilkins' left leg and, recognizing what Taylor intended, the soldier in back grabbed Wilkins' other arm. They lifted him up off the ground and started moving as quickly as they could between the first row of tents.

"We're sitting ducks like this." Wilkins complained.

"Well, sir, our guns weren't doing us any good anyway. Not if we can't shoot anyone now." Taylor said.

"No shit." One of the other soldiers said in agreement.

They kept moving. After a few more minutes they reached the edge of the second line of tents without encountering any other infected soldiers. They stopped and took a brief rest while scanning the open ice that stood between them and the Little Bird.

Wilkins shook his head. "That's a long run carrying me."

Taylor shrugged. "We'll make two rest stops. We'll get it done." The other two soldiers nodded in agreement.

"Those rest stops are going to be in full view of half the camp and no cover." Wilkins said.

Taylor shrugged. "Maybe, but it seems like these boys with the fever can't shoot for shit."

"A lot of them couldn't shoot for shit before they got sick." One of the soldiers said. They all laughed a little at that.

"Maybe so." Wilkins said. "But," he waved at his leg, "even random shots hit something sometimes."

Taylor shrugged again. "I ain't worried about the random shots. Can't stop them. Can't predict them. Can't worry about them."

"Damn straight." One of the soldiers agreed.

"Alright boys, if we're going to do this then let's get to it." Wilkins said.

They nodded and lifted Wilkins back up. A moment later they moved at as brisk a pace as they could out into the open. They covered about twenty yards when a shot rang out. They slid to a stop as one of the soldiers dropped to his knees.

"You hit?" Taylor asked turning to look at the soldier.

The soldier looked back at Taylor puzzled. "Uh...not sure."

Two more shots were fired, but they didn't seem to be close to them.

"That's a sidearm." Wilkins said.

"Hard to hit anything at this distance." Taylor said as they scanned back behind them. They didn't see where the shots were coming from.

The soldier that had fallen slid the backpack off his shoulder. He spun it around and showed the rest of them. He pointed at an entry point into the backpack.

"Didn't penetrate." The soldier said.

Taylor nodded and smiled and then his expression changed. "Shit. The components."

One more shot was fired and then there was a faint sound of clicking. They ignored the shooter now that he was out of rounds.

Taylor dug into the backpack and pulled out a box that held one of the components. It had a hole in it.

"Shit." Taylor said. Then on an impulse he ripped the box open and pulled the component out. He held it up. It was a type of coil about 10 inches in diameter. There was a visible bullet hole right through the box at the point of the center of the coil—-which was nothing more than empty space.

"Well, I'll be damned." Taylor said. He poked around in the bag and found the bullet wedged into the lining of the backpack.

"The son of a bitch felt like someone punched me in the shoulder." The soldier said.

Taylor quickly stuffed the component back into the box and then into the backpack. "Let's go."

Moments later they were on their feet and moving towards the Little Bird again. After another rest stop they stopped next to the Little Bird. They started to lift Wilkins into the helicopter, but he stopped them.

"This won't work." Wilkins said. "Can't bend that damned thing enough to fit inside."

"Looks like you're getting the cheap seat, sir." One of the soldiers said with a smile.

"Enjoy it while you can." Wilkins said returning the smile. They laid Wilkins down on the bench on the outside of the helicopter. They strapped him down.

One soldier circled around and climbed on the bench on the pilot's side. The other soldier happily climbed inside the Little Bird.

Taylor patted Wilkins on the shoulder. "Sorry, sir. There's no beverage service on this flight."

Wilkins shook his head with a smile. "Just fly the damned bird and let's get out of here."

8

Devon poked his head out the door. He scanned the area. Nothing seemed to be moving. He slid out to his right. He carried an XM7 and kept it ready, but he wasn't sure what he would do if someone did start shooting at them. Now that they knew their comrades could be saved they were all reluctant to return fire.

Hernandez came out next followed by Chen. Both of them were from Taylor's group that had already spent time dealing with the infected soldiers at the Main camp.

Devon looked back at Hernandez who gestured towards another building just off to their left. Devon nodded. He crossed an open space and stopped up against the wall of the next building. Chen followed and then Hernandez.

They clustered up closely.

"They seem to just stumble around randomly so we're just going to have to scare one up." Hernandez said.

"Sound draws them to us, doesn't it?" Devon asked.

Chen shrugged. "Sometimes. Sometimes they don't seem to care."

"Well, we need to find one as quick as possible." Devon said. His voice carried a bit of an edge to it.

Hernandez and Chen exchanged a look. They weren't thrilled to have Devon with them. It wasn't because they thought he wasn't capable of doing the job. They were aware at this point of what he had done to get Moreland and Jessica out of the Trench and back here. It was an impressive task.

What worried them was his emotional state. They understood his attachment to Jessica and that her life was now hanging in the balance based on what the major's vaccine could do for whatever guinea pig they could come up with. Everyone knew the clock was ticking.

"Let's move down along the quarters. Less exposure." Chen suggested.

"I like it." Hernandez said.

Devon nodded in agreement.

The three of them turned and moved back past the open space between a couple more buildings. From where they now crouched at the corner of a building they could see the rows of tents where the soldiers were housed. There were two rows of thirty tents on this side of the camp.

One by one they ran across to the gap between the nearest tents. They eased into the space between the rows of tents. They didn't see anyone.

Hernandez nodded to his right. Chen and Devon nodded in agreement. Steadily they worked their way down the row checking left and right at each tent they passed. It seemed like they would reach the end of the row of tents without seeing anyone when a soldier suddenly appeared from around the corner of a tent.

He was holding an M18 pistol, but it just dangled down at his side. They were about ten yards away from the soldier, but it seemed like he couldn't focus on them. It looked as though he had been shot in the lower leg. Not a serious injury.

Hernandez looked at Chen. "Circle."

Chen nodded and ducked back between a couple of tents. Hernandez was two steps ahead of Devon and both of them crouched and watched as the infected soldier slowly shuffled towards them. The infected soldier drew a little closer before Chen appeared from behind him.

Chen grabbed him from behind and Hernandez leaped forward knocking the M18 out of his hand. The infected soldier made a feeble attempt to struggle free, but it took Chen just seconds to secure the soldier's hands behind his back with a nylon strap.

A shot rang out and ripped a hole in a tent next to Devon. He spun around.

"Shit." Devon said. "Where the hell did they come from?"

Shuffling and stumbling along the row of tents were six or seven more infected soldiers. It was obvious to Devon they weren't going back the way they had come with their guinea pig.

Devon looked back at Hernandez and Chen and their captive. "There's nobody behind you. Take him back that way and circle around to the lab. I'll see if I can distract our friends here. That will keep them from ducking back through the tents and blocking you."

"How will you do that?" Hernandez asked.

Devon shrugged. "Don't know yet. Get going."

Hernandez and Chen exchanged a look. They didn't like the idea of leaving Devon behind.

"Go. I'll catch up in a few." Devon said.

"OK. Let's go." Chen said pulling on their captive's arm and half dragging him away. Hernandez grabbed the captive's other arm and the three of them moved back a couple of tents and then turned and disappeared around a corner.

Devon turned back to stare at the approaching soldiers. He wasn't confident that just firing off rounds would keep their interest. Something more dramatic would be nice to hold their attention.

He backed up a couple of tents and then ducked into one. He scanned around the tent for something that he could light on fire. Nothing jumped out at him and he stepped back out of the tent. The infected soldiers were getting closer. Random shots were fired at irregular intervals.

Devon slid into the next tent. There were several liquor bottles lined up on a makeshift table and a bag of pot and a lighter. Apparently these guys were having some fun when the shit hit the fan. Devon glanced at the bottles. He found the one he wanted. 100 proof. He grabbed the bottle of liquor and the lighter and left the tent.

The soldiers were close now. Devon ducked around to the back of the tent row. He moved one tent further and dumped some of the liquor on to backside of the tent and lit it with the lighter. The tent began to burn. The thick tent material produced a dark gray smoke and a nasty smell.

A moment later infected soldiers were shuffling between the tents and nearly at the back where Devon was. They carried a variety of objects which it seemed like they were intent on using as weapons.

Devon turned and ran. He reached the last tent of the tent row. He stopped and poured the rest of the liquor on the tent and lit that as well. He watched the fire consuming the first tent he had lit. Some of the infected soldiers seemed mesmerized by it while others ignored it completely.

Great, Devon thought, they all have their own personalities. That made it difficult to distract them all with one particular thing. Maybe, he hoped, it would be enough.

Devon turned to his left to follow in the direction Chen and Hernandez had gone. He froze. Several more infected soldiers came from around the corner of the front row of tents.

"Shit." Devon said. Worse yet, one of the soldiers coming at him was carrying a 50 caliber. If he started firing that the rounds would shred to pieces the tents and one unlucky Scotty Devon.

Spinning around Devon took off at a run. He had no idea where, as yet, he was going, but he was going there as fast as he could. He had spent very little time in the Main Camp and didn't know how it was laid out.

Ahead of him he saw a vehicle graveyard. Burnt out truck and LMTVs. Clearly fuel from the depot had been spilled out across a wide area and lit. Behind him he heard the 50 caliber started destroying the tent he had lit on fire. Why anyone would try to gun down a fire was odd, but Devon really didn't have time to work that out. Just a true confirmation that these guys weren't thinking straight.

The sound of the 50 caliber was changing and Devon knew that meant the soldier firing it was turning. Moments later he could hear ice chunks being churned up not far behind him. Seconds passed and

Devon could feel pieces of ice hitting the back of his legs. In another second the rounds of the 50 caliber would start tearing his legs out from under him.

He reached the side of one of the burned trucks and without stopping slid under the truck. He somehow imagined that he would slide along the ice under the truck and right out the other side. Unfortunately, the laws of physics did not agree. The ice was partially covered with crusty snow and the friction of it stopped Devon half way under the truck.

Rounds of the 50 caliber started shattering the ice just a foot from Devon. A mist of snow and ice sprayed across him and small chunks of ice stabbed into his face and head. Deon rolled and scrambled as fast as he could to get out the other side of the truck.

As Devon crawled out from under the truck he could hear the clanging of rounds slamming into the other side of the truck. He jumped to his feet and, using the truck as a shield was able to start weaving through the wrecked rows of vehicles.

He kept moving. He wasn't sure how he was going to circle back to the lab or how many infected soldiers might be between him and there, but somehow he was determined to get back to the safety of the lab building and Jessica.

9

"Shit!" Taylor yelled as he struggled to keep control of the Little Bird. The helicopter began wildly swinging back and forth as it approached the Main Camp.

"What happened?" The soldier sitting next to Taylor asked.

"Someone fired at us. We took a couple of rounds in the tail. Blades are fucked up." Taylor answered. He was fighting the controls as the Little Bird was rapidly losing altitude.

"Shit. We're going to hit!" The soldier shouted.

A moment later the helicopter hit the ice. The pilot side landing skid hit first and the Little Bird tipped on to its side and slid along the ice. The main rotor blades chopped at the ice and then broke away. After several long seconds the helicopter stopped. It was tilted to the right resting on the landing skid and what remained of the main rotor blade.

Taylor shook off the shock of the landing. He looked over at the soldier next to him. At first he thought the man was dead. His helmet had cracked the windshield and he wasn't moving. After a moment he noticed the guy stirring.

It took Taylor a few minutes to work himself out of his seat and slide past the soldier to open the door on the right side. He had already tried to open his own door, but it only opened about six inches before hitting the ice.

With minimal assistance from the soldier Taylor was able to get both of them out on to the ice. Taylor laid the man down and turned to look at the bench they had strapped Wilkins to.

"Major?" Taylor called up to the bench that now pointed up towards the sky. It was about seven feet off the ground.

"What the hell kind of landing do you call that?" Wilkins' voice came back.

"Shitty, sir. Some asshole killed our bird." Taylor said. "Let's see if we can get you down from there."

Taylor circled the helicopter to check on the other soldier. There was smoke billowing out of the engine. He could hear the sound of sparks popping up near the main rotor. As he moved a little closer a sick realization came over him. They had landed on that side of the helicopter. Specifically the landing skid and the bench just above it.

One look told Taylor the soldier on the bench didn't survive. His body was twisted and clearly broken. There was streak of blood on the snow covered ice behind them.

"Damn it." Taylor said. He turned away and moved back to stand below the bench Wilkins was strapped to. He stared for a moment and then started climbing up the side of the Little Bird until he was clinging to the side of the helicopter next to Wilkins.

Wilkins looked at Taylor. "Where's your help?"

Taylor shook his head. "One looks like he's got a head injury. Lost the other one."

"Damn." Wilkins said. "Well, get me off here."

"Yes sir." Taylor worked the straps loose and slowly, carefully the two of them got back down to the ice.

Taylor sat Wilkins down on the ice. He moved over to the injured soldier. He eased the man's helmet off. There was cut on the soldier's forehead and his eyes seemed a little unfocused, but he did manage a small smile.

"Might want to work on your landings, Sarge." The soldier said. He seemed to focus for a moment. He looked at the Little Bird. "Bailey?"

Taylor shook his head.

"Damn it. He was an asshole, but he was our asshole." The soldier said.

"Yeah." Taylor said patting the soldier on the shoulder.

Wilkins shifted how he was sitting so he could look back at the helicopter. "Sergeant, you smell that?"

Taylor lifted his head. "Shit. Fuel." Taylor shook the soldier's shoulder. "Get up."

Taylor started over to help Wilkins. Wilkins waved him away.

"Get the parts." Wilkins ordered Taylor.

"Damn. Forgot about those." Taylor said. He spun around and scrambled back into the helicopter. The two boxes lay up against the low side of the Little Bird behind the pilot's seat. Taylor grabbed them and slid back out of the helicopter.

"We need to get away from that thing." Wilkins said as Taylor came over to him.

The other soldier had stood up, but he started leaning severely to his right. Taylor grabbed his shoulder and steadied him. He waited until the soldier seemed to be stable enough for him to let go and then turned back to Wilkins.

Taylor leaned down and helped Wilkins to his feet. Wilkins grimaced in pain. Taylor had an arm around him and they started to move away from the smoking Little Bird. They had only gone a couple of steps when Taylor noticed the stunned soldier just standing in place. He reached back and grabbed the front of the soldier's coat and yanked him forward. The soldier staggered several steps.

Their progress was slow. Taylor shouldered much of Wilkins' weight and kept having to pull the soldier along. The soldier would take a few steps and then seemed to slow down to stand and stare at the ground.

They had only made it a short distance away when the Little Bird blew up. The blast leveled all three of them. It took a full minute before Taylor stirred. He pushed himself up on to his knees.

"Jesus, let go." Taylor said. Taylor could feel someone was gripping the back side of his left shoulder and was squeezing it hard.

Taylor looked over at the soldier and seemed puzzled. The soldier was laying on the ground. His arms and legs were moving slightly, but he was definitely not gripping Taylor's shoulder. When that realization had fully sunk in Taylor twisted his torso around a little so he could get a partially view of his shoulder.

"Son of a bitch." Taylor said. He reached back and pulled a small piece of shrapnel out of his shoulder.

"Help tighten this thing up." Wilkins said.

Taylor turned and saw Wilkins pulling at the bandage around his thigh. Taylor slid over and the two of them got the bandage tight again.

"Can he walk?" Wilkins asked pointing at the soldier.

Taylor shrugged. "Not sure." He saw Wilkins' frustrated expression. "Yeah, I know we need to get the communications up ASAP."

"That's not our only problem." Wilkins said. He waved a hand at something behind Taylor.

Taylor turned and saw numerous infected soldiers slowly trudging towards them from a line of trailers to their left.

"Oh, fuck. This shit's getting old." Taylor said.

"Yeah." Wilkins said. "Get him on his feet. You can't carry both of us."

Taylor turned and slid over to the soldier. He pulled the soldier up to a sitting position. The soldier's eyes remained unfocused. Taylor grab a handful of snow and rubbed it into the soldier's face. It took only about ten seconds before the soldier's hands came up to his face.

"Stop. Stop." The soldier said.

"You need to get on your feet soldier." Taylor said. "We have incoming."

The soldier slowly looked around. He spotted the crowd of infected soldiers plodding towards them.

"OK. OK." The soldier got to his feet.

Taylor lifted Wilkins to his feet.

Wilkins pointed ahead of them, slightly right. "Those out buildings. Let's get there. The communications building is somewhere in that general direction."

"Right." Taylor said. He turned to the soldier. He pointed at the small buildings. "There."

The soldier nodded. "OK. I'm with you."

They moved at what felt like a staggeringly slow pace. Occasionally they heard a shot or two from the approaching infected soldiers, but nothing seemed to be close to them.

When they finally reached the two small buildings they circled around behind them and stopped for a moment.

Taylor was breathing heavily when he set Wilkins down.

"You should get those parts to the communications building now." Wilkins said.

Taylor gave Wilkins a serious look. "No one's getting left behind. It's not that far. A few buildings over. We should get some help when we get close. I left two guys there guarding it."

Wilkins wanted to argument, but he could see it would not get him anywhere and just waste time.

Wilkins took a deep breath. "OK. Then let's get moving."

Taylor nodded. He looked at the soldier next to him. "You good to go?"

The soldier nodded. "Just a walk in the bloody fucking frozen park, right?"

Taylor nodded. "Right."

They got up and started moving on past the small buildings and on toward a larger building ahead. Behind them they could almost hear the shuffling sound of feet. It was an ominous sound.

10

"Where the hell is he?" Chen asked scanning as far as they could see outside the door of the lab building.

Hernandez shook his head. "Don't know." Neither one wanted to suggest that maybe Devon didn't make it. Or that maybe he was laying out on the ice somewhere wounded and dying.

"Shit." Chen pointed. "10 and 2."

Hernandez looked out and saw two groups of infected soldiers moving towards them. He exchanged a look with Chen. They both understood they had about a minute at most before they had to close the door.

There was a groaning sound from the floor behind Hernandez. The soldier they had dragged into the building lay there squirming a little.

"Damn it." Chen said when the minute was up. He pulled the door closed and it banged shut. He flipped a dead bolt and Hernandez helped Chen pile some stuff in front of the door.

"Uh...?" The voice trailed off.

Chen and Hernandez turned around to see Moreland standing behind them.

They looked at Moreland awkwardly. They knew what was coming.

"Where's Scotty?" Moreland asked.

"Um, we separated." Chen said.

"Separated?" Moreland asked. "Why?"

"He was distracting some of the infected guys for us." Hernandez said.

"OK...but where is he?" Moreland asked.

Chen sighed. "We don't know, ma'am. He was supposed to meet us back here."

"And he didn't?" Moreland asked.

Hernandez shook his head. "No ma'am."

Moreland waved a hand at the door. "Well, go find him."

The two soldiers hesitated.

"We...can't do that right now. There's...too many hostiles out there at the moment."

"And we need to get this guy down to Major Mason." Hernandez said. He pointed at the body on the floor.

Moreland barely looked at the soldier laying on the floor. "Scotty could be out there hurt. He might need your help."

"We understand that ma'am, but..." Chen said.

Mason appeared just behind Moreland. He saw the infected soldier slowly wiggling around at Hernandez's feet.

"Why isn't this man being brought down to the lab?" Mason demanded.

"Scotty is still out there. Missing." Moreland said turning to look at Mason.

Mason glanced at Moreland and then back at Chen and Hernandez. "Get this solder down to the lab at once."

"Yes sir." Chen said as both he and Hernandez lifted the soldier off the floor and dragged him down the hall.

"What about Scotty?" Moreland asked.

Mason looked Moreland in the eye. "What about Miss Jessica?"

Moreland opened her mouth and then closed it.

Mason turned and walked away.

In the lab Mason directed Chen and Hernandez to strap the soldier down on to the table.

"He's been shot in the leg." Chen said.

"I saw it." Mason said. "I'll look at that later. First...", Mason reached back and grabbed a syringe, "we have more pressing business. Get his sleeve up."

Hernandez cut the sleeve of the soldier and rolled it back. Mason injected his vaccine into the guy.

Mason looked at Chen and Hernandez. "Get back at the door and watch for Devon."

"Yes sir." Hernandez answered and the two of them left the lab.

Moreland stood a few steps back from the table. "Any idea how long before we know something?"

Mason shook his head a little. "Not really, but he is running a pretty high fever so that might give us gauge on the progress of the vaccine if we see it dropping."

Moreland nodded. She walked out of the lab and into the infirmary. Jessica lay on a bed. Mason had sedated her again.

Moreland put a hand on her forehead. She could feel that Jessica was running a fairly high fever still.

Jessica's eyes opened a little. "Scotty?"

Moreland smiled at Jessica. "He's busy right now. He'll come by to see you in a bit."

"I was dreaming." Jessica said.

"What were you dreaming about?" Moreland asked.

"Digging up bones. In Montana." Jessica said.

"Like you were doing last year?" Moreland asked.

Jessica's face looked puzzled. "Yeah, but then the whole dig site got nuked."

Moreland nodded. "Yeah, well, I've been on some digs that didn't produce much, but no one has ever decided to nuke a dig site." Moreland thought for a moment. "Well, until now."

"There was dust everywhere. A big cloud of dust blowing up into the sky." Jessica said.

"Yeah, I guess that's what it would look...like..." Moreland's mind suddenly shifted.

"Get some rest." Moreland said and then spun around and headed back into the lab.

Mason glanced at Moreland as she walked in.

"If they nuked us, they would nuke the dig site too, right?" Moreland asked.

"What?" Mason turned to look at her.

"The dig site. Would the Army nuke that too?" Moreland asked. Her voice held an edge to it.

Mason nodded. "Yeah. For sure. That's the source of the virus."

"And that would blow the dirt from the site high into the stratosphere." Moreland said.

"Yeah. I guess so. Doctor, what are you asking?" Mason asked.

"The virus is in the dirt and you're going to blow that dirt high into the stratosphere where it could drift for thousands of miles before descending on some other continent." Moreland said.

Mason looked skeptical. "I see what you're saying, but the heat from the detonation should incinerate any virus still out there."

"How big?" Moreland asked. She was thinking though something.

"How big what?" Mason asked.

"How big of a bomb would they drop on it?" Moreland asked.

Mason shrugged. "A tactical nuke. Why?"

"The Trench is about a mile long and based on what we were seeing with the volume of fossils and the USR imaging the entire Trench could potentially contain the virus. Would the heat from a tactical nuke incinerate the entire Trench? End to end? Enough to be sure that no virus would escape into the atmosphere?" Moreland asked.

Mason hesitated. "I...don't know."

Moreland stared at Mason.

"Shit." Mason said. He sighed. "Wilkins damn well better get the communications up."

"Yeah." Moreland said. "Before the Army does something that kills us all."

11

"I don't see them." Taylor said. "Damn it."

Wilkins was breathing a little heavily. "Do you see bodies?"

Taylor shook his head. "No. Nothing."

"I'm going to count that as a good thing." Wilkins said. "How far to the building?"

Taylor took another quick glance at the communications building. "Fifty. Maybe sixty yards."

Wilkins sat on the ice and leaned against the quonset hut they had stopped at. The other soldier had been sitting as well, but he was now leaning far to his left. In another minute he would be laying sprawled out on the ground. The soldier's focus was sporadic at best. Wilkins and Taylor were sure he had a severe concussion. It had been a chore just to get him this far, but it was obvious he would have to be dragged from this point on.

"You've got to take the components yourself. Get them installed and get the satellite connection back up." Wilkins said.

Taylor turned to look at Wilkins.

Wilkins held up a hand. "I know what you said, but headquarters is going to lower the boom on this whole place if they don't hear from us. You've got to go."

Taylor hesitated. He knew Wilkins was right, but he absolutely hated leaving anyone behind. Finally he nodded and then his expression changed suddenly. He was staring at the far end of the quonset hut.

Wilkins twisted around and saw two infected soldiers trudging towards them. One of them was armed and he seemed to be taking aim at them. They were too far away for Taylor to get to them before the soldier started firing.

"Shit." Taylor said. He took a step towards them. He was determined to die trying to take them out if necessary.

"No." Wilkins said. "Go. Get the satellite up. Now."

Again Taylor hesitated. He was paralyzed. He knew what he needed to do, but the thought of leaving his two charges to face what seemed like certain death was stopping him.

Wilkins face was grim. He held up his M18. "I'll kill them if I have to."

Taylor was going to say something when there was a scuffling noise from the direction of the approaching infected soldiers.

Taylor and Wilkins turned to look and watched one of the infected soldiers drop to his knees and then to the ground. The second soldier was still trying to take aim when the butt of a rifle clipped the back of his head and he went down as well.

Taylor and Wilkins found themselves staring at Private Devon.

"Well, I'll be damned. You're everywhere these days." Wilkins said.

"Fucking cavalry." Taylor said.

Devon walked up to them. "Glad to see you guys."

"What the hell are you doing out here?" Wilkins asked. "Is the lab still secure?"

Devon nodded. "I think so. Major Mason needed a guinea pig to test his vaccine on. Chen and Hernandez and I went out and grabbed one. I got separated from them."

Wilkins nodded. "Well, we need to get our asses over to the communications building ASAP."

"Right. What do need me to do?" Devon asked.

Taylor pointed at the soldier laying down next to Wilkins. "You drag his ass over there and I'll get the Major here."

Devon nodded. "Sure Sarge." Devon got a good grip the unconscious soldier while Taylor helped Wilkins get up on his feet.

They moved across the open area that separated them from the communications building. Wilkins was sure, given their luck they would be swarmed by infected soldiers on the crossing, but they saw no one.

At the door Taylor found it locked, bolted from the inside. He pounded on the door. He hoped the locked door meant that someone inside was still alive. "This is Taylor. Open up."

The door swung open almost immediately.

"Good to see a friendly face." The soldier opening the door said. "We had to retreat inside. Too many hostiles."

"Right." Taylor said as they all ducked through the door.

The soldier slammed the door shut and bolted it.

"It's Jennings, right?" Taylor asked the soldier.

Jennings nodded. "Yes sir."

Taylor pulled the two components out of the backpack. He handed them to Jennings. "You know what to do with these, right?"

Jennings looked at them. He smiled at Taylor. "Yes sir."

"Good. Get on it. We need to be up and running ASAP. Got it?" Taylor said.

Jennings nodded. "Right away." Jennings took off down the hall towards the comm room.

Taylor turned to Devon and waved a hand at the soldier he was still holding. "There's a couch in the second room on the right. Put him in there."

Devon nodded and dragged his burden away.

Taylor turned to Wilkins. "We should probably find you a place to rest too."

Wilkins shook his head. "No. As soon as you have the satellite up and running and contact headquarters I will need to talk to them."

"We just need to tell them to hold on the nukes until we see if Mason gets his vaccine working, right?" Taylor said.

"Yeah, but they'll be less push back if it comes from me." Wilkins pointed out.

Taylor thought about that for a second. He nodded. "Yeah. I guess so."

Taylor helped Wilkins down the hall and into to the comm room. He eased Wilkins into a desk chair in the corner.

There were already three soldiers working on the communications console, but Taylor went over to see if there was anything he could help with. It was their only priority now.

It took them another thirty minutes to get the components in and successfully fire up the communications equipment. There was a bit of a cheer when the console lit up and static came out of the speakers.

"Good job, boys." Wilkins said. He rolled his desk chair over to the console and directed them to flip through code book for the right call sign for this day.

A voice returned their call after a couple of tries asking for an ID.

Wilkins leaned over and spoke into the mic. "Chelsea 73."

There was pause before anyone replied. "Confirm ID."

Wilkins repeated. "Chelsea 73."

Another pause. "Stand by."

They waited.

"This is Brigadier General Sanders. Who am I talking to?" Sanders asked.

Wilkins smiled. "General. This Major Wilkins."

"Wilkins?" Sanders asked.

"Yes sir. We were at Richardson together. Alaska. About five years ago, I think." Wilkins said.

Short pause.

"Wilkins. Yes, I remember you. Good God man, you know how close you came to going out in a blaze of glory?" Sanders asked.

"My personal preference, sir, is that you do not nuke the shit out of us." Wilkins said.

"Another ten minutes and the USS Williamsburg would have done just that. So, what's the status?" Sanders asked.

"Major Mason thinks he has a vaccine for the virus. He is testing it now on one of the infected soldiers. We should know in just a little while." Wilkins said.

"Mason?" Sanders asked. He didn't release the mic and everyone in the communications room could hear the muffled sound of someone telling Sanders something about Mason. Sanders released the mic.

"Yes, sir. He's the doctor here." Wilkins said.

"Yeah. I know about him." Sanders said.

There was a pause.

"What's this about a vaccine? I was told our boys were all zombies." Sanders said.

Wilkins took a deep breath before continuing. "Yes sir. We thought that too at first. It seems that Major Mason neglected to inform us that the guys could be cured."

"Jesus Christ." Sanders said. "We were going to kill them all."

"Yes sir...we...killed some ourselves before we knew about it." Wilkins said bitterly.

"God damn it." Again Sanders didn't release the mic. His voice was lower indicating he was not talking to them. "Fucking Mason."

Wilkins didn't say anything.

"Wilkins." Sanders said.

"Yes sir." Wilkins answered.

"You keep this link open and I want to know the results of this test of Mason's. I am sending in some boys to assist you. They will contact you when they get close. You are to take charge of the base. Understood?" Sanders asked.

"Understood, sir." Wilkins said.

"I'll be waiting to hear from you." Sanders said.

"Yes sir." Wilkins said. It was obvious the discussion was over for now.

Wilkins looked at Taylor. "Time for another stroll in the park."

Taylor nodded. "I'll get Devon and the three of us will run the gauntlet again."

Wilkins nodded. "Let's do it."

12

The scream startled Mason and Moreland. They were standing next to the bed Jessica lay in. A second scream got them running back towards the lab. They were greeted by the infected soldier that Mason had given the vaccine to thrashing about on the gurney he was strapped to.

Mason quickly moved next the soldier and felt his forehead.

"Hold him." Mason told Moreland. She moved to the gurney and did her best the keep the soldier from struggling. The soldier screamed again. It was a hideous ear piercing sound.

"What's wrong with him?" Moreland asked.

"Not sure." Mason said as he took the soldier's temperature. "Don't know if this is an expected reaction and everything is OK or...well, if things are taking a bad turn."

The soldier began slamming his head back down on to the gurney. Moreland tried to stop him from giving himself a concussion, but she only managed to nearly get her fingers broken.

The soldier gave out hoarse groan and then fell limply back down on to the gurney. Moreland stared at him for a moment. She was relieved that he had stopped wildly struggling against the restraints, but there was something unnerving about just how calm he suddenly was.

Mason did a quick check and then stepped back and sighed.

"What?" Moreland asked.

"He's dead." Mason said.

"Dead? What...? What does that mean?" Moreland asked.

Mason continued to stare at the body. "It means he's no longer alive."

"Not fucking funny." Moreland said harshly.

"Wasn't meant to be." Mason said.

"Well, what killed him? Did your vaccine kill him?" Moreland demanded.

Mason glanced at Moreland. "I don't know what killed him. If I had to guess I would say he died from a cerebral hemorrhage."

"What caused it?" Moreland said.

"I don't know for sure it *was* a cerebral hemorrhage." Mason. said.

"I know, but what makes you think it was?" Moreland asked.

Mason hesitated. "Because. I wasn't sure to what extent the breakdown of cellular cohesion would take."

"Is that why you didn't want to test it on Jessica?" Moreland asked.

Mason turned back to the table behind him. He began pulling some stuff together as quickly as he could. He seemed to be ignoring Moreland's question.

"I need to scale back a couple of things and then we will need to try it again." Mason said.

"Shit." Moreland said. "Does that mean we need to find another soldier to test this on? We lost Devon trying to get this guy."

Mason had his back to Moreland. He didn't turn around. He shook his head. "No."

Moreland stared at Mason's back. "No? Well, how are you...? Wait, you're going to test your next *best* guess on this thing on Jessica?"

Mason stopped what he was doing. He stood still for a moment and then turned around to look straight at Moreland.

"There isn't any more time. Our clock has run out." Mason said.

Moreland wanted to say something, but she didn't know what. All she could feel was guilt. It felt like the walls of a house collapsing in on her. She had selected Jessica from numerous other students to accompany her here. It was the chance of a lifetime. Now, this wonderful opportunity she had given to Jessica was very likely going to kill her.

Moreland backed up and stumbled into the chair against the wall. She was dizzy. They don't train you for shit like this when you are studying to become a paleontologist. The dead things you are supposed to study closely aren't supposed to be your friends and colleagues.

Mason watched her. He knew she was scared, but he really had nothing except reality to offer her and it seemed like she had already had enough of that for the moment. He turned back to his work.

Moreland sat in the chair leaning forward with her head in her hands. She had no idea how much time had passed. She didn't move until Mason's voice brought her out of the dark place she had slid down into.

"It's time." Mason said.

Moreland looked up. She saw Mason standing in front of her holding a syringe. She felt her guts tighten. She was scared shitless. Slowly she stood up.

Like moving in a dream she followed Mason into the infirmary. The crossed the room to where Jessica lay in a bed.

Moreland stared down at Jessica. She looked pale and it was hard even tell she was breathing. She watched Mason lean over to give her the shot. It felt like she was watching a horror movie on a TV. She felt totally detached from the immediacy of the moment and yet horribly connected to what was happening. It was that little voice from somewhere in the back of her head that kept whispering, in a voice that felt evil, telling her what she was seeing was real.

Moreland felt Mason guiding her to a chair nearby. She could feel the tears start rolling down her cheek. It was the overwhelming fear that she had killed Jessica by bringing her here and it was the total accumulation of the past few days. It was all of it. It rolled right over her in a massive wave and she was drowning in it.

Again time passed. Moreland seemed to just sit in the chair staring at the side of the bed Jessica lay in. There was a small puddle of tears on the concrete floor in front of her.

Mason sat on a bed nearby. He occasionally would get up and check on Jessica's vitals.

More time passed and at the first sound of groaning from Jessica, Moreland jumped up. Mason slid off the bed and joined Moreland at the side of the bed.

"Should you restrain her?" Moreland asked quietly.

Mason shook his head. "No. It either works or it doesn't."

Moreland glanced at Mason. "If...it doesn't work will you need to try again?"

Mason sighed. "If I lowered the ratio any more than it is, well, I don't think this path will work."

"You mean if this doesn't work on Jessica then you've got nothing to stop this?" Moreland asked.

Mason nodded slightly. "Yeah. Pretty much. I would have to start from scratch and...I don't think we have time for that."

"Because your friends will nuke us." Moreland said looking back at Jessica.

"Yeah." Mason said.

Jessica groaned and started restlessly shifting around in the bed.

"It's starting now, isn't it?" Moreland asked still staring down at Jessica.

Mason nodded. "Yeah. Whatever is going to happen, it's going to happen soon."

13

"You have got to be fucking kidding me." Wilkins said. He stared at Devon.

Devon shook his head. "No sir. It works. That is if your aim is good enough."

"And your aim is that good?" Taylor asked.

Devon tried to shrug, but it was nearly impossible with one arm tucked around Wilkins as the three of them maneuvered between a couple of buildings.

"Well, I was a pretty good pitcher in high school." Devon said.

"I'd have to see that to believe it." Wilkins said.

As if on cue ahead of them an infected soldier shuffled into the opening between the buildings. It turned and saw them. It carried an M18 and slowly lifted it up to try to shoot them.

"Hold him." Devon said to Taylor. He released his grip on Wilkins and yanked his gloves off. He scooped up some snow, formed it into a ball, took aim and fired the snowball squarely into the face of the infected soldier. The soldier's head bobbed back slightly and he stopped moving. He seemed stunned and confused. Devon quickly ran up to him punched him. The infected soldier dropped into a pile at Devon's feet.

"Son of a bitch." Wilkins said.

Devon smiled back at them. "I don't know, but it seems to confuse the shit out of them."

Taylor laughed a little. He shook his head.

Devon walked back to Wilkins and slid an arm around him. The three of them edged up to the corner and peeked around it.

Wilkins pointed. "I think the lab is over there."

Taylor nodded. "Yeah. It is."

"Good thing." Wilkins said. "Looks like there's a hell of a fire that way." Wilkins pointed in the opposite direction they were planning on going.

"Uh, yeah. About that." Devon said.

"What?" Wilkins asked.

"I may have burned down a bunch of the housing on that side of the camp." Devon said.

"You did what?" Wilkins asked.

"I was trying to distract some hostiles. Thought maybe a fire might draw them away from Chen and Hernandez. They were escorting our guinea pig back to the lab." Devon explained.

Wilkins sighed. "Well, if we live through this I guess housing will be the least of our worries."

"If we live through this I think I would like to take some leave and find a quiet beach back home. I am sick of cold and ice and cranky people trying to kill me." Taylor said.

"How do you avoid cranky people in Florida?" Wilkins asked.

"Well, that is kind of hard, but it does make wrestling gators seem less stressful." Taylor said.

"I think if we cut around the side of this building we should come out near the side of the lab." Devon said.

Taylor nodded. "Yeah. That should work."

They circled around to the front of the building they had just crept up to. They started down along the front of the building when two infected soldiers appeared at the other end. The soldiers started moving towards them. Neither one of these guys was armed.

"You want to hold the Major I think I can take these two guys out." Devon said.

"Wait." Taylor said. He eased Wilkins over to the side of building so he could support himself leaning against it. Then Taylor took a step out from the building. He raised his XM7 and swung the butt of it over his head. He banged it into the edge of the metal roofing. An avalanche of snow slid down all along the building. It dumped snow down on to the infected soldiers.

The infected soldiers slowly turned in circle staring all around them.

"Hey, what the hell?" Devon said as a pile of snow engulfed him as well.

Taylor laughed and ran down towards the infected soldiers. Within seconds he had dropped both of them. He came back to Devon.

"Sorry, man. Thought you knew what I was doing." Taylor said.

"Obviously not." Devon said shaking himself off.

They gathered Wilkins back up and moved past the end of the building. Sure enough the lab appeared just around the corner. They had to circle the building to get to the correct door, but didn't encounter anyone along the way.

Taylor pounded on the door. "Sergeant Taylor. Open up."

The door swung open almost immediately. Chen looked out at them.

"Glad to see you Sarge. We were hoping it was—-oh, hey, Devon, what the hell?" Chen said.

"Yeah, we picked up a stray along the way." Taylor said.

Hernandez shut the door behind them and bolted it.

Devon looked at Hernandez. "The guinea pig. The vaccine test. Did it work?"

Hernandez shrugged. "Don't know yet. We heard some screaming down the hall earlier, but no idea what the status is."

Devon handed Wilkins off to Hernandez and ducked down the hall. The infirmary was closer than the lab was and he reached the door of that first. When he looked in he froze.

Moreland was draped over Jessica as she lay in bed. Moreland was crying. Mason stood back a few steps.

"Oh, my God, no." Devon said. He took a shaky step into the room.

Mason turned to look at him. His face was expressionless.

Moreland lifted herself up off of Jessica and turned to look at Devon with red eyes.

Devon got a look at Jessica. She was pale.

Jessica turned her head and smiled at Devon. "Hey, soldier."

Devon crossed over to Jessica and hugged her.

"It works. The vaccine works." Moreland said to Devon as he leaned over Jessica.

"I would feel better about the result of you didn't sound so surprised." Mason said.

Jessica looked up at Devon. "I dreamed of Pittsburgh."

"What?" Devon asked. He looked over at Moreland.

Moreland shook her head. "You probably want to ignore that."

Devon stood up. Something occurred to him. He turned to Mason. "Major Wilkins. He was shot back at the upper camp. I think he needs you."

"He was with you?" Mason asked.

Devon nodded. "Yes sir. Found them by the communications building."

"Did they stop the nukes?" Moreland asked.

Devon nodded. "Yeah. A General Sanderson stopped the launch and is sending some troops in."

"Sanderson." Mason said sourly. "I know him."

"How...close was it? Before they nuked us?" Moreland asked.

Devon looked at her. "About ten minutes."

"Holy shit." Moreland said.

Mason nodded and turned. He walked to the door of the infirmary.

"Get Wilkins down here." Mason yelled down the hall.

"Sir?" Devon asked.

Mason looked back at Devon. "Yeah?"

"Is she going to be OK now?" Devon asked. He glanced at Jessica.

Mason nodded. "Yeah, she's going to be OK. All of us are."

Epilogue

1

Wilkins stood watching the scene. The sound was deafening. There were detonations going off all along the edge of the Trench. Massive chunks of ice dropped down into the Trench. Eventually, when enough of the ice had been reduced to rubble, huge bulldozers would begin pushing the piles of ice further and further out into the Trench.

General Sanderson stood next to Wilkins watching the work. It would take a while, but, ultimately, there would be no trench at all. It would just one large field of broken and jagged ice. An uninviting place that needed to stay uninviting. The plan would be to surround the final rugged ice field with razor wire and signs ordering anyone and everyone to stay away.

"Still would have rather nuked the damned thing." Sanderson said.

Wilkins shrugged. "Sounded like that was going too be risky. We couldn't be sure we didn't blow the damned virus all over the place."

"Maybe so." Sanderson said. His silver hair and his face were about the only things sticking out of his bulky overcoat.

"Sir?" Wilkins said.

"Yeah?" Sanderson glanced over at Wilkins.

"I heard Mason was being sent back to the States." Wilkins said.

Sanderson nodded. "He is."

There was moment of pause before Wilkins spoke again. "To work at DARPA again?"

Sanderson hesitated. Personnel assignments at DARPA were considered confidential, but he knew immediately where Wilkins was going with his question.

"Yes." Sanderson said.

Another pause.

"I am having difficulty letting go of his actions here." Wilkins said.

"You mean specifically on withholding information about the infected soldiers." Sanderson said.

"Yes sir." Wilkins said. He huffed. "Sir, we were killing our own. Soldiers we knew and cared about."

Sanderson sighed. "I know. And you are thinking that Mason is not facing any disciplinary action for it."

"Yes sir." Wilkins scuffled his feet in the snow. "We should have been told at the onset what we were dealing with. We would have found a way to work around killing them."

"Are you sure?" Sanderson asked. "They were armed and they were, at that point, hostiles. Are you certain you could have avoided killing any of them?"

Wilkins hesitated. He wasn't certain. "I couldn't promise you that we could have saved every one of them, but we could have spared some. He should have told us."

"And in trying not harm the infected soldiers you would increase the risk of losing more of your uninfected ones, correct?" Sanderson asked.

Wilkins hesitated. He didn't really want to answer that. "Possibly."

"You think Mason's getting off easy." Sanderson said.

"Yes sir." Wilkins said.

"Major Mason is going back to DARPA to work on thoroughly define this virus. He has the most experience in it at the moment. Did Mason tell you why he was shipped down here?" Sanderson asked.

"He said that the pressure at DARPA was too high. He didn't like what he was working on." Wilkins said.

Sanderson smiled. A small smile that had a certain disdain to it. "The pressure on Mason at DARPA was to keep him working on the projects he was tasked with. Mason wanted to work on his own pet projects. That's a hard no at DARPA. People cannot just play around with whatever strikes their fancy at DARPA. Not in the department Mason was in. Mason was having trouble following the rules. This is the Army. People don't make their own rules. That's the pressure he was feeling there."

"And you're putting him back there?" Wilkins asked.

"Major Mason is going to find this assignment at DARPA comes with much stricter controls, tightened oversight and a constant keeper to monitor all of his time there." Sanderson said looking over at Wilkins.

A small smile crossed Wilkins face. "You mean he's going to hate it there."

Sanderson smiled at Wilkins. "This is the Army, not summer camp."

"Go where you're ordered to, do what you're ordered to do." Wilkins said.

Sanderson watched another blast go off and nodded.

They were silent for a couple of minutes.

"You are staying here until this task is complete, correct?" Sanderson asked.

"Yes sir." Wilkins added.

"I have not checked the status of the men." Sanderson said.

Wilkins knew what he meant. "I believe they have nearly all received the vaccine now."

They both were quiet. Similar thoughts ran through each of them.

"Any count on how many we lost?" Sanderson asked.

Wilkins shrugged. "Hard to say. Some of the bodies were difficult to determine who they were and then matching that our records. I was told we lost about 60% of our personnel."

"Damn." Sanderson said quietly.

"Yeah." Wilkins said.

More explosions rumbled towards them from further along the Trench.

"Did they give you a revised estimate on when this will be completed?" Sanderson asked.

Wilkins shook his head. "No. Nothing more than a general timeline, but I will stay here and watch this until the whole damned thing is buried. Hopefully forever. And then, I guess, they tell me I have earned some leave."

"Yes, you have." Sanderson agreed. "Any plans for your time off?"

Wilkins shrugged. "Don't know. Maybe I'll go to Florida and learn to wrestle gators."

Sanderson glanced over at Wilkins. He smiled again and shook his head. "Whatever."

2

"A fucking B?" Jessica said.

The other five students in the grad class almost seemed to cringe. There was almost always someone in any given class unhappy with an exam grade, but, as a general rule, no one made a scene in front of the professor.

"What?" Moreland asked. She was leaning back in her desk chair at the front of the room.

"You almost killed me and now—-this? A fucking B?" Jessica said. She held up the paper.

The other students seemed to quickly segue from awkward tension to excited viewers. They had been waiting for this through the first half of the semester. Neither Jessica nor Moreland had talked much about the trip to the Antarctic. Their abrupt return. The military escort they had received. Nothing said.

Jessica refused to talk about it. Moreland shut down any discussion of it. The University was saying nothing. The lack of answers to questions and general silence was bizarre to say the least. They now suddenly realized that it was all about to come spilling out.

"I didn't almost kill you." Moreland replied. "As a matter fact, I believe you were the one that nearly shot me."

Every eye of the other students widened. Sure enough. This was going to blow up right in front of them and they had the best seats.

"That stupid M whatevery gun jumps all around when you shoot it. And...and I was trying to save your ass from a zombie." Jessica said. She waved the paper in the air again. "And then this. A fucking B."

Jimmie Reston's mouth dropped open. He loved zombie movies. "Oh my God, zombies." He whispered to Emily next to him.

Emily slapped him on the shoulder. "Shh! There's more."

"The way you were shooting you could have taken out the whole damned camp." Moreland said. "And I didn't need your help. I believe your exact words about me were 'zombie killing bitch.'"

"Oh shit." Susan grabbed Dan's shirt. "Dr. Moreland's a bad ass."

Dan nodded. "A zombie killing bad ass."

Moreland heard that comment. She thought she should say something to squash that kind of talk, but, somehow, she couldn't bring herself to do that.

"Yeah, well that was after I saved everyone on the ice wall." Jessica said. She slapped the paper down on to the desk.

"What? You were the one falling over the edge." Moreland said.

"If I had fallen I would have dragged the two of you with me." Jessica said proudly.

"You saved yourself with a fork." Moreland said.

Jimmie's brow furrowed. He looked at Dan. Dan returned the puzzled expression and slowly shook his head.

"No fucking clue, buddy." Dan said.

Jessica glanced around the room with a smile and nodded. She pointed at herself. "That's right. The fucking ice climbing queen."

"Anyway, it wasn't my fault you almost became a murderous zombie." Moreland said.

Jimmie suddenly looked at Jessica in a completely new light. "Wow, I would love to have zombie girlfriend."

Jessica gave Jimmie a disgusted look. "Yuck. And, by the way, my boyfriend is bad ass soldier in the Army. So eat shit."

Suddenly Moreland realized that they had lost all sense of composure and secrecy concerning their Antarctic adventure. She looked at her watch. "OK. We're done here for today."

Jimmie raised his hand.

Moreland had started to gather up some things on her desk. She stopped. "You have a question about hip structures in the early Jurassic, Jimmie?"

Jimmie shook his head. "No, Doctor. Did the zombies have to be shot directly in the head?"

Moreland stared at Jimmie for a moment. "That...is not a paleontological question." She shook her head and went back to gathering up papers on her desk. She saw Dan's hand go up.

Moreland sighed. Her hands froze in place as she eyed Dan. "Please tell me your question has something to do with early dinosaur skeletal structures."

Dan shook his head. "No Doctor. I'm confused about the fork on the ice wall thing."

"Oh my fucking God." Moreland slapped a file folder on her desk closed. "OK. We're done here. Please just go. Oh, and I am canceling my office hours for the rest of the week."

Slowly and reluctantly the students collected their things and filed out of the room. Only Jessica remained.

Moreland and Jessica looked at one another.

"You got a B because you can't remember anatomy for shit." Moreland said.

Jessica frowned and then thought about it. She snickered. "Yeah. That's probably true."

They both sat quietly for a moment.

Jessica's expression turned dark. "Doc, how do you forget something like that?"

"Anatomy?" Moreland asked.

Jessica shook her head. Her expression was serious. "You know what I mean. The whole damned thing."

Moreland shook her head slowly. "I don't know. Honestly, I don't think you can."

They sat in silence for a minute again.

"Are you trying to forget it?" Moreland asked.

Jessica shrugged. "I don't know. I think I would like to, but I guess that's probably not going to happen. I still have nightmares, though."

Moreland nodded. "So do I."

Again the room was silent for another minute.

Moreland looked at Jessica. "I...promised myself I wouldn't mention this to you. After...everything that happened down there, but...I have an opportunity to do some work in South America. In the Amazon."

Jessica's face lit up. "Really? Wait, are there zombies?"

Moreland smiled. "No. No zombies. But...there are some aboriginal people that may not be happy we are there, potential drug cartel people that would happily kill us and a host of tropical diseases."

Jessica pretended to think about it. "Well, Scotty isn't going to have any leave for the next six months. I guess I could squeeze it into my schedule."

Moreland nodded.

"Are you sure you want me along?" Jessica asked. "After all," she held up her exam paper, "I'm only a B student."

Moreland smiled. "Wouldn't take anyone else. What if I came across an ice wall?"

Jessica smiled and nodded. She pointed a thumb back at her chest. "Fucking ice climbing queen."

Moreland placed a hand on her own chest. "And zombie killing bitch."

K McConnell
kmcconnellbooks.com
kmcconnell@kmcconnellbooks.com

Don't miss out!

Visit the website below and you can sign up to receive emails whenever K McConnell publishes a new book. There's no charge and no obligation.

https://books2read.com/r/B-A-CGLDB-IRMCF

BOOKS 2 READ

Connecting independent readers to independent writers.

Also by K McConnell

Office of Scientific Operations
Office of Scientific Operations - Release #1

The Hamlet Mysteries
The Hamlet Mysteries 3

Standalone
A Conspiracy in Blood
Symbiotic Puppets
The Plague
The Club of the Bombastic Few
The Master Switch
Hamlet On A Budget
The New Sheriff
Office of Scientific Operations - Declassified Files (Release #2)
Office of Scientific Operations Release #3
Office of Scientific Operations - Declassified Files (Release #4)
The Hamlet Mysteries 1
Office of Scientific Operations - Declassified Files (Release #5)
The Hamlet Mysteries 2

Office of Scientific Operations - Release #6
The Hamlet Mysteries 1 - 9
The Trench of the Dead

Watch for more at www.kmcconnellbooks.com.